Seven Fish Tree

Seven Fish Tree

Ron Shaw

Cover concept, design, and creation by author, Ron Shaw

Published in the United States of America
ISBN13: 978-1-62329-060-3
ISBN: 1-62329-060-0
Mercer Publications & Ministries, Inc.
Fiction / Visionary & Metaphysical

Contents

Prologue

I am Rod Travis, and what follows was given to me as in a waking dream some seventy-two hours ago.

Shortly, you will find I am no professional writer or accomplished author. For my evident shortcomings in this medium contained on the pages to follow, Humbly, I do apologize.

I have been compelled by an unexplainable force to write what you will read here.

Call it what you will.

Take it or leave it as you will.

Is it purely a cautionary tale or a rare opportunity to see what will occur? I do not know.

I have no rational understanding or explanations why at this time in the waning years of my life this endeavor has become such an urgent necessity.

Since the first day of receiving the initial message, my life has been consumed with what you will read.

These last few days, it has become the sole priority in my existence.

The words are mine only in they are restricted by my vocabulary and lack of writing skills.

For me, a first time writer, the hectic pace of writing this must have been inspired by someone or something beyond me. Typically I am not this motivated.

Are any of the images portrayed in this book real or true? Yes.

Are these happenings destined to come?

Are they signs which have been shown to others beyond me?

Are the dates provided real deadlines?

If not, were the dates merely shown as being urgent for their impact or effect?

Is the outside force I refer to a true sign?

Better still, could these signs be a direct result of the overall feelings of futility many in America are experiencing these days? Does the unrest we see across the globe play a part in these dire messages?

How long can mankind survive like this? Is this the question which drives me here?

Am I simply an old man seeking the truth while resting alone on a park bench?

At this juncture, I neither have the answers to these questions nor have I been provided a title for this morose manuscript.

I am certain the title will come soon — from whom or from where, I cannot say. But with certainty, I can also say it will be revealed to me and not created by me.

As much as any manuscript can be said to be, this one is finished, and I pray the force which has consumed and compelled me for these last few days is satisfied... at least minimally.

One of the questions above has been answered. The title was given to me, appearing as a mental interruption during an unrelated family conversation. Like everything else you'll find on the following pages, it also arrived in mysterious fashion by the same voice, compelling me to write this story.

Genesis

And Jesus said, "The person is like a wise fisherman who
cast his net into the sea and drew it up from the sea full
of little fish. Among them the wise fisherman discovered a
fine large fish. He threw all the little fish back into the sea,
and easily chose the large fish. Anyone here with two good
ears had better listen!"

—Gospel of Thomas 8 (sv)

S uddenly, I awoke, standing in the middle of a large field...
mesmerized, staring at the most magnificent tree I had
ever seen. It was massive! The giant tree rested in the
center of a large tract of open land composed of softly rolling
hills carpeted with lush green grass. Vibrant colorful flowers
dotted the Oz-like landscape. In the distance, hardwood trees
lined the circular field.

The pastoral track reminded me of those rolling fields I'd seen
in a popular children's TV show a few years earlier, *The Teletubies*.
It was no less striking than the green golf fairways at the Masters
Tournament in Augusta, Georgia. However, the tree demanded
the majority of my attention.

Obviously, it was hundreds of years old or maybe thousands,
judging by its size alone. The trunk's diameter was the second
most impressive aspect of it. Its main lower limbs ran almost
perpendicular to the ground for about one-tenth of its height.

They grew shorter as they turned more towards the heavens to the top.

I could not adequately guess how tall it was. While standing some thirty yards from it, my neck could go back no farther, gazing at its top. Most of the limbs I could see could have easily been trees on their own.

The tree was not symmetrical in appearance, and its obvious weight and size did not seem to burden or strain it. Oddly, the words "pure perfection" came to mind.

Its leaves were just as unique as their host. In sixty two years, I had never seen leaves or a tree like this one. I had no clue what type of a tree it was, but in metro Atlanta, the possibilities were some-what limited. The leaves were larger and more lush than those of a maple, oak, or pecan, but they were somewhat similar in shape in a combined way. This was strange.

The tree appeared as if it belonged in parts of Africa, the tropics, or rain forests. The color of its leaves reminded me of dark green ivy which is prevalent in Georgia. The leaves glistened beneath the clear fall sky... as if sprinkled with thin ice.

At this time, it struck me as odd none of its leaves had a fall look. Not one leaf had fallen to the ground... neither had any grass changed or flowers in the field shown signs of dying for this time of year and the coming winter.

The size of the tree's trunk was mind-boggling. If a cross sec-tion was provided at its widest point, one would need a lot of time, patience, and a calculator to count the age rings. The bark of the tree was a dark coal color. It was somewhat smooth which was also unusual to me for such a tree. It reminded me of the texture of an elephant's skin in a coal color with the same glassy appearance of a newly chipped piece of coal.

There was a light afternoon breeze, and as the leaves lazily swayed in the wind, the entirety of the tree glistened with a mu-ted sound like a Georgia pine forest on a windy day... music for your entire soul. In the light favorable breeze, the tree also had a detectable scent which some trees like pine and sassafras have.

I couldn't quite put a finger on a singular scent, but with my eyes closed and a big nasal inhale, several sweet fragrances came to mind like the aroma of a newborn baby's skin and hair, the scent of freshly sliced vanilla beans, a juicy ripe pineapple when cut fresh, or the interior of a new car. It was those and more.

As these aromas titillated my nose, palate, and lungs, I heard a slight coughing sound coming from behind me — then again louder and a third time even more forceful. It was painful to look away, but I did. A few yards to my rear there was an occupied park bench which I hadn't noticed earlier. A young man was seated there, staring up at this tree. Maybe, he had quietly appeared and sat on the bench while I was studying the huge tree. Nonetheless, I was surprised at both.

Walking over, I stated, "Mind if I have a seat?"

At which, he replied, "Not at all, have a sit."

I was twice his age and nervous. I was uncertain as to how he had appeared undetected. It was perplexing. He was clean-shaven with dishwater blond hair. The short-haired young man was neat in appearance and casually dressed. I decided he must be in his mid or early thirties. Guessing a person's age and weight were two of the limited things I could do. Due to his overall demeanor and body language, sliding over and smiling, he now looked older to me.

Obviously, he was at ease and exuded a peaceful presence. His smile appeared genuine and somewhat fixed which I later determined to be two of his numerous positive character traits.

The man wore blue jeans, tennis shoes, and a short-sleeved plaid shirt in grays. There was an old Georgia Tech baseball cap resting beside him on the bench. He was a pleasant-looking young man. He wore no watch, making me like him even more.

"Thanks, what a beautiful day. Some tree, eh?" I commented.

Initially, we began slowly by mainly talking to ourselves with repeated praises for this tree and the entire area. We were cordial, but he was more guarded in what and how much he said. I added wise to my cursory assessment of him.

As usual, I could not stop jabbering after the initial ice was broken. Soon, I hijacked the conversation like a preteen with a new discovery or toy. The young man didn't appear to mind. Thankfully, I caught myself and geared it back. This is when he took over the conversation, and his next words would mark the precise moment my life began its transformation. My already strange day was about to morph into the most bizarre one ever.

Your life will also change... it's inevitable.

Turning his attention to me on the bench, the man stared me in my eyes and said, "Rod, let's start over. I should properly introduce myself. I'm Jonathan Huna, but my friends throughout the centuries have always called me Jon," extending his right hand for an introductory shake.

Answering with a jovial smile, "Very nice to meet you, Jonathan, but I don't think I told you my name was Rod — but it is, and my friends also call me Whale... but only for decades."

The shadow of the tree engulfed us.

"How did you guess it?" I stated, as I firmly took his hand and we shook.

"Please, Mr. Travis, call me Jon," he said.

"Only if you call me Rod," I answered. He knew my last name as well. This weird day became intriguing.

"Mr. Travis, I mean Rod, I have a story to tell you as well as a business offer with possibly a miracle thrown into the mix. You are perfectly welcome to turn all three down, but if you listen to the story with faith and belief in a stranger, you will take my offer. At minimum, listen to an excellent true story and I think — no, I am certain — you'll take my business offer. I must warn you the story is free, yet partial, but the offer and potential miracle are not. I'll add, in life, nothing is really free and cost is relative. I will also admit the offer is affordable on paper while the promised miracle may cost you. It has cost me everything and nothing. I would gladly pay a million times over for the experience," he said.

At this point, intrigue didn't capture what I felt. Questions ran through my mind, "Is this guy insane? Is he serious? Could he be more mysterious, cryptic, or interesting?" He looked and sounded perfectly sincere and if not, what an acting job, what talent! Naturally, I had to hear more.

With a Cheshire cat grin on my animated face, I said, "I accept. Please, do proceed, sir."

"We will need to discuss some conditions and revelations as there are plenty of both at each phase of this process. They'll be revealed to you on a time-specific and a need-to-know basis. Do you understand this?" he responded.

This elevated my interest to new heights, and I replied, "Yes, I understand or suppose I do or as much as I can understand without knowing anything substantial yet."

He responded, "First, briefly, allow me tell you my story. This will answer many of your questions. It will also provide a few of the initial revelations and basic conditions of which I spoke.

"I was born in what is now upstate New York in the Year of Our Lord 1533 to Mr. and Mrs. John Huna. I am four hundred and eighty years old. We were a pioneer family. I lived on our farm within a short walk of the Hudson River with my parents for thirty hard, yet wonderful, years.

"My early education was handled by both of my parents in the home. My parents were well educated in England. They came to the new world for a different future. I was born in this new world.

"At the age of thirty, four hundred and fifty years ago, I was given an opportunity for a new and different life. On a rare day off from the farm, I was fishing on the Hudson River when I first saw this same tree and parcel of land near where I fished. I had caught a stringer of catfish for the family. My attention was turned to a sound of laughter behind me, coming from inside the tree line. Upon inspection, I was led by the laughter to this same field and tree you now see before you.

13

"Rod, I sat and watched your demeanor from the moment you appeared here before this tree. Believe me, in 1563, I had similar feelings and reactions about its grandeur. Like you, I did not notice the man sitting behind me as I stared frozen at the tree... until he laughed robustly again. Our meeting went along the same course as mine and yours today. Inexplicably, the old man knew my name before we met, and he also knew how many fish I had caught.

"He made the same pitch to me of a story, an offer, and a miracle with conditions and revelations. At the time, to me, he seemed totally harmless and genuine. Simultaneously, he appeared otherworldly, strange, and yet, special. I have to repeat, he made me the same offer you will receive and with all the stipulations attached within the totality of the deal.

"I was offered the ownership of this tree, a miracle tree, and this parcel of land for the small price of my day's catch — minus the twelve fish my family would need for their supper.

"If I agreed to the deal, he further advised the tree would reveal to me what it required of me like it had done for him. He could not speak of what the tree had revealed to him except he was to meet me at this location on this day with the three-pronged deal. Rod, I later determined my agreement was as pre-destined as yours.

"This sounded too bizarre. At least mentally, I had to take a step back and consider the pros and cons. The land was valuable, the tree was valuable, and the miracle may be even more so. I could tell no one, not even my parents. The tree would let me know when and what I could say in respect to this transaction.

"Trust me, Rod. This is the single most important transaction you will ever make and no doubt, the most important one in history. For me, it has turned out to be such and much more.

"With all of the good and bad considered, I remained somewhat hesitant.

"When he received the fish as payment in full, my seller advised he would sign over the paperwork. The paperwork was rolled-up inside his jacket pocket. I later found it listed me as the current sole owner of this tree and property. He also advised the paperwork dates back to the original owner. This should have led to more questions from me, but at this juncture, internally, I wrestled with how to do this — if I should do it.

"I had caught nineteen catfish this day, but they were running small. He didn't mind. I gave him his seven fish, but I asked if I could run the other twelve home to mom and dad. They were waiting for my catch for supper. I would come right back for the paperwork. Smiling, he stated, 'Hurry back and don't tell anyone' Rod, he appeared to have no doubts about me or this transaction taking place.

"I raced home, handing the fish to mom. She insisted I skin and gut them before returning to the river. I told mom the fish were biting well and for them not to wait for me for supper. I ran back to the field. Beneath the tree, the old man was waiting. I startled him for an instant when I appeared in a hurried huff. He signed the paperwork and turned it over to me to sign. I did so.

"At this juncture, he said, 'The tree and property are all yours.'

"He added, 'Remember, you must always do what the tree advises you to do and to the letter. You can never harm the tree or this plot of land in any way. It will forever be just as you see it today... now, you're the guardian.'

"He reached out his hand and we shook, closing the deal. As we stood beneath the branches, he said, 'Goodbye. Now, look up into your tree.'

Jon continued, "That is when the miracle occurred. No quicker than I'd looked up, I returned. I was back inside my body. I recalled the man's eyes twinkled, and he smiled widely as he said, 'Goodbye.' Together, we gazed up into the big tree. Bewildered, for a moment, I stood there. The old man gave me a last wave, and he was gone. Shortly thereafter, the tree advised what it required of me, and it has done so at every phase of my life to this day, to this place, and to this meeting for four hundred and fifty years. At this time, this is all I can divulge."

Needless to say, I had a giant migraine headache filled with questions, running through my brain. I thought, "You didn't tell me about the miracle.

"What a fantastic story... what miracle?

"What else have you done for so many years?

"If I buy this tree, will I live as many years?

"What about your parents?

"Financially, how did you survive throughout the centuries?

"Did the tree and land provide for you and if so, how?

"Why did it need guardians?

"If I accepted, what does the future hold for me, this tree, and this land?

"Am I also destined for this guardianship?"

"Jonathan knows I'll accept anything he proposes.

"The possibilities are endless.

"The responsibilities could literally become impossible." These additional thoughts also pounded my throbbing mind.

Suddenly, the tree loomed much larger.

Changing of the Guard

After Jon had finished his story, an excited silence existed between us for several long minutes. During this silence, I know he saw the dumbfounded and irritated look of confusion on my face as questions riddled my mind.

Suddenly, I blurted out, "Wait a minute. Hold on. How can you leave it like this? What... ?"

"Rod," he interrupted, "just as I had reacted before you, I know you have plenty of questions. Some can be answered now between us, but as I said earlier, things will be revealed to you in their own good time. There are certain restrictions placed on me which cannot and will not be broken by me at any time. I have remained diligent and faithful for all these years, carrying out every instruction given to me. Selfless obedience is paramount. You also will be instructed as to these requirements.

"For instance, I can tell you this tree and surrounding landscape are the same as I bought with seven small catfish centuries ago. Yes, it was originally located in upstate New York when I became its guardian. 'Guardian' is emphasized here, Rod. The tree does not belong to me or even to you when you pay the fee and agree to take it over.

"By the time I leave you, you will know all the answers to the very core of your soul. I can also tell you it is the largest and oldest tree on this planet. What you see with the eye or mind is not necessarily all you see or think. It is the greatest tree in the whole

17

universe. It is as old as time itself. Don't allow this to confuse
or overly perplex you... not yet. Ultimately, this too will be explained to you.

"You and your partners must and will agree not to attempt
to harm this sacred land and tree in any way. You can't damage
it. It will not burn, and it is impervious to earthly elements which
routinely age or damage all other living things. Be assured, it
is alive. I know it is eternal. The tree and grounds are miraculous but not magical. In its presence, we're on hallowed ground.
There is nothing fake, mystical, or magical about it or any of this.
It is a guardianship more akin to a pleasant responsibility.

"I have said your life will be changed forever. Believe it. There
is no way to tell if you will live hundreds of years like I have or
live normal lives. You will not know in advance what the tree
will have scheduled for you four. Some of the future has been
revealed, but the total of which I have no knowledge. Knowledge
is also a key component of this duty you are offered.

"As you can imagine, education, knowledge, reading, and writing have been lifelong vocations of mine. How much could you
read or write if you'd lived four hundred and eighty years? In this
regard, understand writers, philosophers, mathematicians, phy-
sicists, geniuses, gurus, saints, and sinners throughout the history of man have strived to learn what this tree will give you in
half a breath. Literature is replete with pieces of this whole.

"Soon, you will have questions about God, religion, Heaven,
life, death, hell, good, evil, the soul, spirituality, creation, the universe, and infinitely more — you're human, and why shouldn't you?

"But please take some of the sagest advice in the last half millennium and don't over think it. Its brilliance lies in its simplicity,
and in less than twenty-four hours, all of your questions will be
answered. Like me and all of the guardians before us, questions
breed more questions.

"Okay, I will throw you a bone. Here's the biggest answer you
seek. What is the miracle? After all, I am the oldest living man

thanks to the tree. Think about this for a few seconds. Try to imagine how many amazing and incredible things I've seen come into existence in my lifetime. Now, multiply all of these by Pi, and they will still pale in comparison to what was revealed to me near the banks of the Hudson in 1563.

"Rod, this tree is life! The easiest answer is the miracle is real, and once we conclude the deal, it will be greater than anything you can imagine. Over the centuries, from what I was told and learned, each experience is and will be somewhat different. The best way to approach or understand this cryptic answer is to recall what I have said all along. The task you've been chosen for will be revealed to you as mine was for me. Only the tree knows when instructions will be given.

"Each guardian has become an integral part of the whole. We will be with each other for eternity. Carl Sagan was surely correct. 'We are all made of star stuff.' I would add, a few have, do, and will shine brighter for their obedient works."

"Work is another key word to this sale. Forever, mankind has strived to be better — to do more. A form of payment or reward for ones good work is part of man's DNA. It is primal as well as innate. This is why payment is required for this to happen. Payment, good work, and rewards, how simple is this, Rod?

"Does this answer some of your questions?" Jon ended.

"Certainly, it answers some of them, but may I ask a few more?" I responded.

"Sure, but just a few because we're on the clock you know," he exclaimed, presenting a huge smile.

I said, "Okay, first, how about your parents? Did you leave home immediately or could you postpone leaving?"

"From the moment the seller and I shook hands and we looked up into the tree, I never saw my parents in person again, but I have been with them as surely as I am now with you. My parents were religious, as am I, believing in God and Jesus Christ as Our Savior, but one of the beauties of the tree... sorry,

I apologize. At this juncture, I cannot go there. Suffice to say, through their faith, eventually, they were comforted and at peace with my absence. It was made known to them I was fine... living, prosperous, and on a spiritual mission. Readily, they could believe, understand, and appreciate this.

"Remember, it was an important life mission which brought us to this land," he answered.

"Have you ever been sick, seriously injured, or ill?" I asked.

"No, well yes, before the event. You are learning already. After my miracle was shown, I have not been sick, ill, wounded, or injured. Will I live forever? Yes! Will you, or better yet, do you expect to?" Jon responded.

This answer intrigued me, but I did not pursue it.

"Jon, earlier, you mentioned 'my partners,' 'you all,' 'the four of you,' and '24 hours to pay.' What do these mean?" I asked.

He simply smiled. "Let's get down to the money, Rod," he said.

"Sure," I answered.

"Your cost for this will be one thousand US dollars in cash," he stated.

I knew I only had two hundred and fifty dollars on me to use for this, and it wasn't enough. So, I tried to bargain a little with him and asked, "Would you accept less?"

Laughing loudly, he said, "No way, big spender."

"Why are you laughing?" I responded.

He said, "I tried the same thing with the fish, and 'No way, big spender,' my seller answered without even a chuckle.

"Rod, you're a good man or else we would have never met. I know you are thinking of offering three friends a quarter each of this transaction. It will be fine, and I knew about it. Your three friends you immediately thought of will do it for you on faith alone... but you know this. 'Faith' is also an integral part of the foundation of this entire endeavor. They will do it for you, but before this happens, there are several additional conditions."

I thought, "How does he know these things? Is it part of the tree's power or information?" Predestination came to my mind instantly as I recalled Jon had said I was "predestined" to accept the deal. As shocking as it might seem, I was at complete peace with the prospect."

"Just how much do you know? Can you read my mind? Jon, are you like Merlin, living your life backwards or something?" I said.

He also had a big chuckle at these questions and responded, "At least, this will be a little fun for me and of no substantive harm. So, think again of your three friends, and we will see what happens."

I thought, "I will ask Barry, Matt, and Jim for financial help." These men were three of my dearest friends.

He exclaimed, "Yes, they'll do it, and from the last one you thought of to the first, you call them Pops, the Ringer, and Big!"

My jaw dropped towards my lap. He knew their nicknames.

"Rod, you have until 4 PM tomorrow to meet me with the money. Come by yourself. You are to tell no one about me, the substance, numerous conditions, and revelations of this deal. Don't tell Rose and Faye."

There he goes again. How does he know these things?

"Your three friends can only be told they are investing in real property, consisting of land and a tree for which you are to be the guardian. Do not say owner because in reality, none of you will own anything. I know you can persuade them to invest. Tell them its future is invaluable, and you'll all prosper beyond your wildest expectations. Let them know they will have to play central roles in the stewardship of this joint purchase, but you are and will forever be the principle or guardian. They'll be equally important stewards or equal stock holders. All of these statements are true. I'll see you back here before the deadline tomorrow," Jon Huna advised.

I left the field with Jonathan still seated on the bench, staring at his tree... correction, at the tree. He did not own it either. How I got home I cannot remember. Mentally, I was still somewhere in the clouds when I suddenly but figuratively, fell full force to the pavement. My feelings of euphoria were now visions of dread. My faith was being tested. Was this man for real? Was I being played for a fool, a simpleton? Should I even call my friends? My mind and body sank into despair.

Inexplicably, the movie *Field of Dreams* came to me and a booming voice in my mind said, "They will help." It was on again.

I cannot lie or mislead you. The thoughts of development, monetary prosperity, and financial gain ran rampant through my head like those brave stupid souls running from the bulls each year in Spain. What was to come? I did not know, but prosperity sounded good just about now. For the last few years, financially, times had been tough for me and my family. Family members were losing their jobs, houses, furniture, and other personal possessions. We tried to help as much as possible, but now our bills were becoming harder and harder to pay. The bottom line was we needed a magic tree in our life. I forgot, it is not magic, and this should never cross my mind again. Honestly, we could use a miracle or two.

I called my three friends, and each fell into the deal as predicted by Jonathan. But he hadn't mentioned how much grief and jokes came with the money. We were on a conference line at the same time, and each had his moments of poking the stick at me in a corner.

They would win either way it went down. If it failed, they had me for life as an idiot, but if it was true, they would prosper as I would. What else did I expect? We were the best of friends, and guys, thank you for always being there for me.

Money Changer

B y noon the next day, the funds had been obtained. It was no easy task to keep my friends away. During the evening and morning, the three friends pled for more information or at least a hint at where and when the money would change hands. I was adamant and warned to comply fully with the instructions given to me by Jonathan Huna.

The drive to the property was about twenty minutes from my house. I made it in ten minutes. It was 12:30 PM when I walked up to Jonathan, sitting on the park bench. His initial overall manor and clothing were different today. Things seemed a tad askew for both of us. My nerves were about shot. His face and voice were stressed, but it was easily understood. He was retiring after so many centuries on the job. In consideration of the importance of his works, it was a miracle he was in control of himself on any level.

I sat beside him and said, "Good afternoon, Jonathan."

"Good day to you, Mr. Travis. I assume you have the money?" he stated.

"Yes, as you directed but before we conclude this, there're a few hundred questions I would like to ask you," I responded.

His smile came back to his face as he answered, "Certainly, Mr. Travis."

"You have said the tree will provide for us as it has provided for you, and all my questions will be answered in due time by either you or the tree. Is this correct?" I inquired.

"That's right. Except, the tree will provide most of the answers you continue to seek — as well as any future inquiries as to the tasks for you and your friends, once they are revealed. Of course, the how, when, and why of this will be at the tree's discretion," he replied.

"Alright, it is simple enough. But what about my life now, my family, and my day-to-day routine? After all, you immediately left family, hearth, and home at thirty when the miracle was presented to you. This scares me the most. I hope you understand this and can provide some comfort for me in these regards. For instance, how did you provide for yourself all those years? Where did you live? Were you required to live your life alone all those centuries?" I stated.

There was a brief hesitation in his answers. Possibly, too many questions were asked at once or maybe, the answers were too severe or too painful for him to consider and easily respond.

"What happened to me was required of me through my instructions. Leaving my family was the hardest thing I have ever done to this day, but after the miracle, there was never any hesitation. The tree will tell you and your friends what is required of each of you. This is not known by me.

"In 1563, I was told I would write for my livelihood. So, at the tender age of thirty, I began the most prolific writing career in the history of man... all the while guarding this portal. Trust me on this, Rod, I was no writer, but quickly and consistently, the words came to me. They were provided.

"Rod, maybe the time will come when you are told to write. Are you prepared? Are you a writer? If not, do not worry. All will be given to you.

"I've written and published thousands upon thousands of articles, short stories, novels, poems, novellas, music, newspaper articles, plays, graffiti in Paris, and even haiku on occasion. Everything I have authored has been under pen names. I'm the ultimate ghostwriter.

"I was also tasked to travel the world. I have done so many times over but always on a mission. It has been a busy and most lucrative guardianship. The money for support question is of no consequence. Do not worry about money. One leaf on the tree before us is more valuable than all the wealth I've accumulated in centuries. Money is no measure of our value. We are not judged by our monetary wealth or possessions.

"In twenty five of the cities I have recently visited, accounts have been set up with the names of your friends and the others who will join us in the near future.

"You will choose some of the twenty one who will come next. These funds all over the world will be vitally important. Rod, your monetary needs have also been handled.

"This reminds me, these last two days have been the first time I've traveled without pens, pencils, and paper in hand or pocket. I feel naked before the tree and humbled by the magnificence of a wonderful life — thankfully, one of duty and purpose coming to its end. I envy you and your three friends, Mr. Travis. I rejoice at all of our futures. Yours are just beginning and mine at journey's end," he stated.

At this moment, Jon produced an leather-wrapped roll of parchment, containing more than a few old yellowed pages with ragged edges. It looked ancient. He advised the pages contained the names and dates of sale for each transaction of this property from the beginning. I didn't know from what beginning.

1563 was the last year of recorded transfer. He told me there would be plenty of time for me to study the documents, and they would be as he had advised, "most interesting and revealing."

He fumbled in his shirt pocket for a pen he had forgotten. After a laugh, he asked if I had one. I did and he presented an open palm to me for the money. I counted the one hundred dollar bills into his hand, and he folded them once, pocketing the one thousand dollars.

Then, he signed the document over to me, and in turn, I signed it as the sole owner of the property. There was a brief legal statement above our signatures and dates, explaining the legalities of the transfer and the rights of possession from the signing until its transfer or resell.

At this point, he added, "I forgot to mention it, but this land and tree cannot be willed, given away, bartered for, or traded to anyone else. You are now the sole owner of this. You'll maintain it as directed for as long as directed in the manner as instructed until such time your instructions are to sell it to a named person or persons for a predetermined fee. Your friends will be able to experience the miracle and hear this story on the date specified by either me or the tree. Do you understand and agree to all of this?"

I replied, "I do."

Jonathan stood up and walked over to the tree, standing under the massive lower branches. I sat watching his every move. For a brief moment, he looked up into the tree and nodded in the affirmative. He waived for me to join him beneath the tree, and he quipped, "Ready for a miracle?"

Before I could say yes, Jonathan took my left hand in his right and said, "Look up into the tree with me."

Together, we did so.

Miraculous!

As I gazed up into the branches of the tree, within a nana second or less, my being, or at least my mind and consciousness, shot up into the tree. First, I witnessed my life from conception to birth to this day. Literally, I saw and heard every second of my life go by to date. My mother's womb had to be as close to Heaven as one could get. I had never felt such warmth, love, and tranquility. To this day, her heartbeat echoes softly in my mind.

There was nothing but the good presented to me. There was none of the sadness, hurt, or pain we experience in life. My life had been perfect in this replay. It was exactly like others have described during a near death experience when their lives flash before their eyes in a second.

My replay brought me to this day to the moment Jonathan and I looked into the tree. As quickly as my life came, it left.

At this point, I had no feelings of motion or any aspect of my body. But for some odd reason, I did know it was there. Through my mind, I felt everything which was happening within my being. I was shown the emotions, laughter, and experiences with my loved ones. Absolutely everything imaginable was presented.

Next, I felt and saw a bright bluish-green light flash over my being as if it were probing for something. In half of a wink, it was gone. I began to ping and pong from limb to limb... up, down, and sideways throughout the tree.

As this was occurring, my mind became a massive computer, and I was aware of every bit of sight and sound, entering my brain. To date, the world's history was made known to me from the beginning of the universe. It wasn't at all like a Cliff Notes version. It was more akin to a thorough Collegiate Britannica Encyclopedia version with modern updates. In its entirety, this downloaded into my brain as easily as you can get a song from iTunes on your iPad.

Believe me, I know how impossible and bizarre this sounds, but it doesn't negate the fact it happened.

The entire time this was going on, I zipped from limb to limb like a subsonic jet, all the while feeling no motion or gravity. Exactly right... there was no gravity during this experience. The tree was a vacuum to me.

Similar to my life, the history of our world was filled with only positive images and sounds. As well as other human sufferings, wars were made known to me, but not in a negative light. For example, all wars were documented using heroic acts of the victors. Through the good deeds done by man for man, the soldiers liberated cities and countries — ultimately, as most in the world celebrated wars ending. The bad things in history, which had to be shown, were editorialized by emphasizing only the positive. I was appreciative of the method used.

Shooting from limb to limb, time seemed to be vacant here. It was pleasant and fun. With each leap, I could feel myself changing.

The endorphins in my brain were intense. Soothing feelings of euphoria swept over my mind and weightless body like muffled rolling thunder. They seemed as if they'd never end.

My other senses were also energized — the floral and spice fragrance of the tree and the pace and ease of my flow coexisted with the knowledge everything was streaming visually in the highest definition and resolution in 3D I've ever seen. All of this was phenomenal. As it was occurring, this entire experience was intoxicating.

When the history segment ended, I was whisked to the top
of the tree. I was aware I was standing there at treetop. This
was the first time I was made aware of the rest of my body.
Briefly, I peered down from the top. At any other time of my life,
this would've freaked me out since heights aren't my best friends.
This time, there was no fear or apprehension in the downward
glance. These feelings of content, warmth, security, and even love
were indescribable.

It was at this point I realized for the first time I was breathing.

With a huge smile, I gazed into the heavens. As I did so, I
shot upward not unlike Superman as he rockets from Earth. I
was flying. Within the slightest fraction of a second, I was rocketing through the universe, passing galaxies like they were sec-
tions of a city sidewalk straddled with every large step. I jetted
past moons, planets, star clusters, suns, novas, black holes... a
supernova was occurring and much more.

We are so tiny.

I was one with the fabric of the universe. I had a complete
panoramic view of it all as it passed by me. This was too much.
I was certain I was going to explode, or at minimum to implode,
before I could see and experience all of this beauty.

For the first time, my tears flowed, streaming down my cheeks.
At least, the tears confirmed gravity was present within my body
space, but who cared. For me, this experience was a dream
come true. As a young boy and into adulthood, I had often asked
"why" while peering into the heavens. I've held a lifelong love for
matters concerning the universe, our wondrous blue planet, and
the miracles occurring here and out there.

Thank you, God!

With the thought of God, the surroundings changed. I can
only describe the next experience as being in a tube or hole like
a water slide whose exterior walls were opaque, yet gaseous in
appearance. I could see colors and what appeared to be faded

red and orange lightning bolts, streaking in all directions on the outside of the tube. The tunnel was remarkably linear or straight in appearance.

This leg of my journey appeared to last a long while until a drastic change occurred. A pitch black opening appeared at the end of the tube. In a snap, I was dispatched into the blackness of nothingness, and there was no feeling of movement, mentally or physically. This was the first time in all of these wonders I was somewhat afraid or at least concerned. Panic crept into my mind.

Mentally, this horrid feeling evaporated as quickly as it had appeared. Straight ahead, I could see a small bright penlight in the distant blackness. This vibrant light grew rapidly, and in an instant, I was engulfed by a warm and soothing blanket of white. It reminded me of my mother's womb but brighter.

This sea of white consumed me, and I loved basking in it. Its warmth and smoothness could actually be felt like a clean white sheet fresh from the dryer, draping across my arms and face.

This had to be Heaven. I thought, "Leave me here, and all will be fine." Through the years, I'd heard and read many times about this white light from lots of people who had near death experiences. It was and is a common phenomenon. Yet, all of these people returned to life from the experience which occurred while unconscious from injury, massive coronary, stroke, or while under anesthesia. I was here — alive and yes, this had to be Heaven.

At this precise instant, I understood how those fictional baseball players of yore felt when they crossed onto the baseball field from the cornfield and then, back into them in the film *Field of Dreams*. "Build it and they will come" sprang into my head for the second time.

I had come.

At this thought, the white lifted like a wispy cloud on a sunny day, and I witnessed it evaporate.

It is humanly impossible to adequately describe what was before me, but I'll attempt to do my best.

As I approached this place, I saw it was huge and alive but without any signs of man or beast. The entirety of the planet, or whatever it was, was gently glistening as if the air was composed of light pleasant-to-the-senses glitter — or tiny ice particles rather than oxygen.

Think of all the religious pastoral scenes you have viewed in art or discovered in literature, and minimally, you will begin to see what was before me. There were bright sandy beaches. Striking the sand, the ocean's blue water was as gentle as a summer's breeze across your face. There was little or no tide.

In some way, the landscape was different. It was as a patchwork of mismatched scenery and various landscapes. In the distance, there were majestic waterfalls, and rolling hills covered in grass like below at my field. Huge trees with similar plots such as mine could be seen dotting the countryside as far as the eye can see.

Every visual thing here was inviting. There was absolutely nothing unpleasing to the eye or senses. In fact, its aroma was the same as my tree... simply sublime. I could see no signs of life here or in the distance, but for some reason, I could feel a presence or beings. It was difficult to explain, but something or someone was out there. I felt no harm would come to me. I knew this.

I looked behind me and saw the most beautiful pink and robin's egg blue sky I'd seen. The heavens here seemed close to you as if you could reach up and touch them. There was a huge pale blue planet resting at 12:00 and a galaxy just to its left. A cluster of moons and planets were off to the distant right. A soothing muted sun appeared to float at the waterline.

When I looked back, instantly, I was standing on the beach. Oddly, I could leave no footprints when I walked on the sparkling sand. I could feel the sugar like sand beneath my feet and toes.

I walked to my right down the beach a few yards. The sand reminded me of the sand at Navarre Beach in Florida. To my immediate left, small sand dunes ran parallel to the beach. The tallest dune I saw was about four feet high.

The dunes were sparsely covered with a tall and angular plant, resembling sea oats or pampas grass. The plants had a three-petal purple flower situated at the top of the stems. The purple flowers resembled aged trilliums atop sea oats. These plants were swaying in a warm breeze, flowing from inland towards the open sea.

In a beautiful way, this area resembled the oceanfront Federal Park tract which runs along the beach and ocean from Navarre Beach to Pensacola Beach, Florida.

Between the dunes, I spotted an open path which led to what looked like a floating oasis. Growing closer to the lush oasis, I saw it was suspended above the grass-covered ground just beyond the beach and dunes. In disbelief, I stared at this for a time. It was as magnificent as anything I had seen while here. From a thicket of palm trees at the edge of the oasis, I could see what appeared to be semi-transparent ghostly forms — shapeless bodies moving towards me. They resembled upright mirages. As they floated nearer to me, their shapes began to take form.

Without effort, they glided from the oasis to the grass near me. I could see who they were. Randy, our nephew, was first to greet me. Tragically, Randy had died fourteen years ago at the age of twenty-four. I grabbed our Randy, hugging him with all my might. Tears covered my face. I kissed his rosy cheeks. Next, my grandfather, Papa, who died in 1968, appeared. We embraced like we had many times in the 1960s. Then, my mother, Ann, appeared beside Papa and next, my grandmother, Nanny. I embraced each of them one at a time and then, all together. There were plenty of kisses to go around. Lastly, my mother-in-law, father-in-law, and my wife's grandfather were there.

To this point, we had not spoken. Suddenly, I missed Rose and Faye. They should be here beside me. Finally, I tried to speak. In the blink of an eye, I was back, standing beneath the tree, looking up into the branches. I was covered in tears with my mouth wide open.

"Not fair! Not fair!" I screamed.

Jonathan walked over from the bench and tried to console me.

"How long was I gone?" trying to compose myself, I asked, wiping the tears from my eyes, cheeks, and neck.

He said, "When you looked up and took a breath, you returned before you exhaled your breath."

"This is impossible — no way, Jon. You were beside me, and then, you were on the bench when I came back. It had to take you longer than half a breath to do this. Didn't it?"

"All is possible," he briefly replied.

He took me by the left elbow, leading me over to the bench. We sat down, and he advised we had plenty to discuss. Time as we think we know it would be one of the first discussions.

I was exhausted and decided to take a short rest. We sat there, staring at the tree together in silence for fifteen minutes or so. My stare had become a thousand mile one.

Why couldn't I have stayed there? Why raced through my mind. Answers do breed more questions, and my brain was overwhelmed.

Energy Flows Where Attention Goes

"I don't know, Jonathan. I just don't know. Maybe, you have chosen the wrong person for this job. I'm not worthy. This is too much, too fast, and I still haven't been advised what my tasks will be," I lamented.

After another short pause, I continued, "I was standing there in my bare feet, and I don't know why I was shoeless on a beach in Paradise. I was right there, Jonathan, and more overwhelmingly happy and content than I have ever been, rejoicing with my family... my dead ones. It was the ultimate homecoming which should have lasted an eternity. Yet, in an instant, I was plummeted to the depths of sadness and despair. I was expelled from Heaven to a bottomless abyss in a flash, and none of the endorphins could help. Icarus's plummet to Earth had to be easier.

"Jon, when we first met and you began telling me your story, rather, your fantastical yarn, I thought it was entertaining, and you appeared to me to be a nice enough guy with an inner calm which kept me at ease. I have to admit my first impression of you was you were missing a few roof shingles. By the minute, it became easier to believe in you and have faith in all of this. After all, the tree and landscape are real.

"Everybody could use a miracle in their life. I could. I also thought maybe I was chosen because we were both Christians.

34

Now, it's apparent to me one's spirituality or particular religious inclination has nothing to do with this. Jon, if I'm wrong, will you let me know?"

"No, Mr. Travis, you're not wrong," he stated.

"In addition to the many revelations given during my journey, it is apparent in some substantial ways I have evolved," I added.

Jonathan's answer to this was presented telepathically as his mouth and lips didn't move. In my mind, I heard his short answer, "correct."

Then, with voice, he said, "Rod, for the time being we'll communicate in the usual way, but be assured this entire conversation between us could be handled without uttering one word verbally and in considerably less time and less effort.

"Early only in your journey through the tree, did you experience the bright probing light? If so, internally, you have been changed in marvelous ways. Also, a few exterior improvements were made. Both of us can thank the tree."

He continued, "I know exactly how low you feel, but have faith this confusion will pass quickly. The same feelings and more overwhelmed me beneath this tree in 1563. I also fell like a rock from grace in the midst of my homecoming in the hereafter.

"I had to leave a young wife and maybe, a child who journeyed together to our Lord in the year 1559. You are more mature with more life behind you than I had seen in only thirty years. I also knew what was lost in an instant, experiencing the feelings of unworthiness and inadequacy.

"There was so much information and an uncertain future filled with grave responsibilities. By this point, any task would have been too much for me. Every cell of my being wanted to bolt to my parents and the farm. I wanted to hide.

"This had to be a bad nightmare or a vexing, and my guide into this craziness was immediately summoned to the tree. He was gone. I had no place to run and nobody to answer my questions. Today, for reasons not yet fully made known to me, I was told to stay for a while longer to assist you and the twenty four in the mission.

"There was plenty of work to be done, and time was growing shorter by the hour. This is why you saw me on the bench when you returned to your body. I was looking forward to my last trip to the treetop and my last task. I ached for my family and the beach where my footprints would finally be seen. I'd waited for this far too long. Rod, I am consumed by this sadness we share."

"Wait a second, Jon. You said 'assist you and the twenty four.' What twenty four? Soon there will be five of us when Pops, Big, and Ringer arrive, and you may leave at any time, right?" I said.

Jon replied, "We will get into the math a little later. I can see the twinkle has returned to your eyes, and I detect a perplexed smile. I assume the endorphins have come alive again. Yep, I see they have. By the way, get used to them. They are here to stay.

"How's your eyesight?" he stated, "No need to respond it is at minimum 15/15, and also, you will find your night to be exceptional. Each eye has independent macro as well as zoom capacities. Next, check your hearing, and you should find the sounds you hear can be mentally amplified. Do you hear the cat in the far tree line to the right edge of the field? If not, concentrate and you will hear it. Remember, your new hearing capabilities can also be a problem. Many things will require adjustments up or down. Play with it a bit, and you'll begin to appreciate it.

"Are you feeling any pains in your joints or anywhere else on your body? I know you aren't. Be careful when you go home and interact with family and friends because these gifts are for you. It is not time to reveal any of this to your friends or loved ones. Jim, Matt, and Barry will soon discover these things. Your wife will see a pleasant improvement in your libido. Try to act normally like you did before the improvements.

"Next, I want you to open your mind and clear it of all thoughts. Think of the blackness before you came into the white light. Now, concentrate on the soothing light and recall any of the scenes you were shown during your life's history or history itself. You should be able to 'see' it totally like you uploaded it to your brain.

"Okay, think of another and another and another. All four or five should be running concurrently in your mind. There is no limit to the number of windows you can open in your brain now. Multitasking mentally is my favorite.

"When you signed the paperwork, I noticed you were right-handed. Well, now, you are ambidextrous? Did you see the films *The Matrix, The Terminator, Continuum, Blade Runner, or AI?*

"If so, you'll come to know Hollywood has nothing on our maker.

"Before you met me and afterwards, took the journey, you used only about ten percent of your brain. This is normal for most humans. The greatest thinkers in history used a higher percentage of their brains but not much more. Now, we can utilize ninety-nine percent of our brains. From all reports, the last one percent would either catapult us back to the apes or elevate us closer to God.

"Before all of this, you and I believed in God and Paradise. Here is the heady stuff. You and I are the only two people on Earth who actually know they both exist. We've seen, felt, and inhaled it — we alone walk this planet with exceptional exclusive gifts from God. I fear we're both blessed and cursed. Lest your head swells too much, there's plenty of hard work ahead. I never said it would be easy."

While Jonathan talked, I was playing with my new toys. My body, mind, and soul had never felt as good, and yet, outwardly, I looked and felt the same. I realized my soul was as prevalent as my arms or fingers. It engulfed my mind and body, tingling me ever so slightly from head to toe. It was soothing and pleasant.

I smiled and winked at Jonathan. He returned the gestures.

I was ready.

We were ready.

Now Is the Moment of Power

"Things will begin to happen more quickly now, Rod. In a few minutes, you will phone each of your partners, instructing them to meet you here early tomorrow morning. Like clockwork, they will answer and come.

"We need to discuss what you and I can advise Jim, Barry, and Matt before they experience the miracle. The pre-journey information they're to be given must be much less than I have thus far provided you. This has been ordered. Naturally, we want them to be at ease. So, at first, allow the discussion between the four of you to occur as normally as possible. Be cautious as to what you reveal about the tree.

"I will wait on the backside of the trunk for a while to give you a period to become at ease with each other. Then, at the right point, I will join you. Let me make the introductions. Before we make the calls, there are a few more things we must discuss," Jon advised.

Jon continued, "For instance, do not be fooled with a feeling of familiarity with the tree and its power. Like I have said, it can quickly become intoxicating, especially to those of little faith. This is 'the Tree of the Knowledge' as described in the Old Testament, and impure sources will tempt you in its name. Call them what you will, but today, they are surely poisonous fruit or vipers as they were then. There are some within the twenty four whose faith is weak, but with diligence and supervision we, more accurately you, can handle this.

"There should be no mystery as to why you four were chosen. All of you are retired. Two are ex-police supervisors with many years of experience within a major metropolitan police department. One is a true genius, artist, musician, prolific reader, and writer. He is possibly a savant who is extremely spiritual in many ways. The last member is also an artist with ample experience in business and supervision. You will find the other twenty one will have similar traits.

"Rod, the best have been picked, but like us, none are perfect. You should know this since you have inadvertently, chosen a few of them. I will explain the twenty four in depth to you and your friends once they've had the full experience.

"They will also share in our improvements. Telepathic communication in the near future will be vital in your tasks. Failure in any way is not an option. As we speak, there are deadlines approaching, and time is short.

"You're encouraged to use the tree when needed. Take the trip again and again. Be advised, the journey may change in a minor or significant way on each excursion. Each use will take about the same amount of time — a second or two at the outside.

"I told you I would explain the time issue to you. Rod, activate your search engine... our Creator's Google in your brain. Upload these publications in this order, *The Creative Mind, How the Universe Works, The Erte' Story, Creative Dreaming, The Fourth Way, and last, Hawaiian Huna.*

"Basically, the time conundrum is simple. Different planes exist. When we sleep and dream, it is a well know fact the actual time of the individual dream or dreams we have is only seconds in real time. The dream seems like it lasted a long time with plenty of activities which normally, would consume more time.

"For example, your total trip to Paradise and back only lasted about a second in real time. During yours, I moved to our bench to demonstrate two separate time planes exist. Look at it another way, in essence, as you entered the tree and returned, your second of time was almost frozen. You were permitted to travel within another plane.

"In this other plane, a human second can seem like a lifetime. I was able to enter the tree with you and immediately, return to the bench while you traveled... my increased brain function. Like the fact you'll never be ill or unhealthy again, this ability was also given to you when your brain was rebooted. You can stop the yearly flu shots.

"As I related, at some point, the voice will reveal itself to you as to your mission, and this will be accomplished in whatever fashion it chooses. Who is the voice? I will leave this to your personal interpretation. I took mine to be the voice of God. Maybe, it wasn't, or it was by use of another vessel. You'll understand this when the time comes. It is an individual thing just for you and me. The access will be different for the others.

"Jim, Barry, and Matt will not be given orders like us. Theirs will be passed along to them by us. For now, we're the last to hear the voice. You and I are the guardians. Rod, your role will be much greater than mine has been, or I believe it will be. I don't envy you or those who follow your path. The twenty four to come will be the ushers to carry out our instructions.

"This is worth reiterating — one's personal religious beliefs, spirituality, or total lack thereof are of no concern in our endeavors. We will soon serve all of humanity.

"That's enough for now," he ended.

"Enough?" I quipped, rhetorically, in front of a nervous chuckle.

"We need to move more quickly as 'things will move faster now'? Are you kidding me? Do you realize I met you yesterday... less than than twenty-four hours ago? Things are going to speed-up? Are you serious?" I added.

"Absolutely, all of those are correct. Know this though, I've almost known you a lifetime... a 'your kind of' lifetime, Rod!

"Now, tell me in a few minutes about each of your friends since I don't know half of their stories. But first, get them on the phone, giving each these instructions — provide our GPS location on the bench, advise them the tree's location is close to Atlanta which will let them know they have a short drive, tell them it will be much better if they come here together in one vehicle, they are expected by 9 AM tomorrow, and direct the three to follow the dirt part of the road until it dead ends.

"They will see your vehicle, and another one or two may be there, seeing how people love to walk these woods for exercise. It will cover my vehicle's presence for them. Tell Jim they're to follow the deer path at their 9:00 position, if they park straight in towards the big oak at the road's end. I know Jim is the hunter, and he'll have no problem with this. Advise him you know he's going to suggest placing a deer stand or two in the tree for the season, but tell him he cannot. It is strictly prohibited. This should cook his noodle a bit. Tell them to follow the deer path for about sixty yards or so and then, to the given GPS coordinates. This is important. End the call by saying it is imperative they meet these requirements and abruptly, hang up. Jim will call you back, but advise him you knew this and to just follow the instructions, Pops," Jonathan instructed.

"What is the importance of the GPS stuff ?" I said to Jon.

"Rod, those are the instructions which were given to me for you and the three. The GPS coordinates will give Pops a chance to show off his new internet phone to Big and Ringer. He will be able to navigate their way here using his GPS system on his phone. As an added attraction for me and maybe you, it will be humorous. Verbally, they'll pounce you for the cryptic nature of these orders.

"Rod, I will tell you this in advance. Each of your three friends will be given the task of supervising seven people to assist in the coming mission. Each will be provided a list of seven by me and you.

"You and they will know many on the list but not all. In fact, you will assist more in the selection of some of them. There will be both men and women chosen. All are retired. They are exceptional and have led exemplary lives of caring and servitude to their fellow man. Each will agree immediately but one. They'll be given the miracle. All will be advised what their tasks will be, and they'll gladly perform them.

"As I have done, they also will leave family, hearth, and home. You will too. They will learn all will be provided. They are not to worry about sustenance, clothing, or money. Everything will be given.

"They will be ushers and ordered to travel to distant lands. What we see before us will be there for them when they arrive. They will be responsible for an identical 'garden' like we have here.

"Other pertinent information will be given when needed. My time is growing short. Home is where I yearn to be, but as directed, I will do what is required of me.

"Now, tell me a little about Barry 'Big' Prat, Jim 'Pops' Warner, and Matt 'The Ringer' Ringer? They sound interesting," he stated.

The Second Guardian

"Jonathan, before I get started on my three friends, tell me what exactly you meant, 'you have known me for a lifetime.' What do you know about me?" I stated.

"Rod, it is really what you might expect. Many years ago, the voice with the help of the tree made known to me about your birth and life to come. Just as you and I were shown our life histories on the limbs, yours was shown to me. At the time, I was advised what I was to do to prepare the way for you.

"Throughout the years, my tasks became more and more targeted towards preparations for you, your friends, and the twenty one to come. It was only yesterday when my assignment changed, and new information was provided about the others we will soon bring into the operation.

"Firstly, though, I was shown your history. Your birth in 1951 at Crawford Long Hospital in Atlanta. I'd add to date the bill has not been paid for your birth.

"After seeing these events, you have led a remarkable life, but somehow I doubt you would believe this statement.

"I saw your early childhood years and all of the difficulties inflicted upon your mother, your siblings, and you due to circumstances totally beyond your control.

"I saw your father, who was never really part of his family, walk out on your mother and her four children when you were six years old.

"I witnessed an event before this. In the dead of night, your mom dragged you small children to a brothel on Bankhead Highway to confront your father's lover who ran the place. It was a frigid night. I witnessed the results of this encounter.

"David, your older brother shot rocks with a slingshot at the windows. You threw larger stones at the house.

"Your mother cried, begging your father to come home with you five. You needed food and the bills had to be paid or else you would be thrown into the streets. This was a common theme for you all.

"This night, a verbal ruckus ensued. Profanities laden with threats of physical harm flew from the two-story brothel like hornets disturbed from the nest. He hid at first. Then, your father chimed in with orders and more profanities. I recall 'damned kids' being said a lot by his mistress, her daughters, and him. He refused to come home.

"Late at night, on a busy highway, you small children and your mom had to walk miles back to an apartment without heat and without food.

"I also saw the time just before your dad left for good. In the dog days of summer, your mother and you four kids started out on foot, traveling to the far end of Bankhead Highway to its intersection with Fulton Industrial Boulevard. At minimum, it was a six mile walk each way.

"An Atlanta police officer in a squad car stopped you about half way there, asking your mother what she was doing out in the heat with these small children. Ann explained to him you were trying to find your father, and someone had told her where he was. He was with a girlfriend, and reportedly, they were in a black car selling produce at this intersection. The policeman loaded you in his police cruiser and drove there. Y'all found your father with a woman, trying to sell produce. The fruits and vegetables were all over the hood, roof, and trunk of their car.

"It was a miserably hot day. Harold, your dad and his girl-friend had opened all the car doors and windows. Harold re-clined on the front seat with his head in the woman's lap. His feet were hanging out the opened door. She sat in the driver's seat.

"Y'all were told to stay in the police car while the officer han-dled this. I know you recall what the officer first said to your dad. I don't think you know exactly what was said before the officer cold cocked him with a right haymaker, laying him out cold.

"First, the officer asked him if it was his wife and four chil-dren in his patrol car. Harold said, 'Sure, what of it?' The officer told him to get out of the car, and go home with your family. He replied, 'No.' At this moment, his girlfriend chimed in, 'Hell no, Harold.' Rod, you heard this. The officer moved in closer, facing your father while yanking from the car. Next, the policeman said and I quote, 'You've got to be one sorry son of a bitch,' and then, he knocked him out. You were impressed.

"The officer drove you home and advised your mom to file for divorce. He was able to provide information about family services where she could receive help without cost.

"I saw the financial devastation which followed.

"I witnessed the time you, as a young boy, were on the *Popeye Club* show on WSB TV in Atlanta. While your mom, sister, and younger brother watched you win the Simon Says game, men came into your rented house and collected the rental furniture had initially come with the house. None of the bills had been paid. Your sorry father was always missing. Your sister Lynn cried and pleaded for the workers not to take the television, advising them her brother was on this show.

"I saw you on the TV show wrapped in yellow soiled bandages, covering your arms, legs, parts of your neck, and face. These ban-dages protected the oozing wounds of poison ivy which riddled your body. You remain highly allergic to sumac, poison oak, and poison ivy.

"I also witnessed the times in the mornings when your mom and grandmother had to pour water on you to unstick your open wounds from the sheets which formed during the previous night's sleep. I saw you as a small boy in the hospital having surgical procedures to remove the numerous scabs covering your body.

"Later in the evening, when you returned home from the TV show, I saw you had received two small bags of treats from the show. One was for the game win and one everyone received for attending the show. This was your family's supper this night — a 12-ounce can of Pepsi Cola, a small bag of Gordon's Potato Chips, a dozen Colonial Brown and Serve rolls, a twin pack of Colonial Cream-filled Cupcakes, and a Bonomo's Turkish Taffy candy bar. These were split equally five ways between you. After the furniture was removed, your older brother returned home. Your mother didn't eat most of her share. She gave her food in equal portions to you and your siblings.

"I saw all of your Christmases come and go. Often, there were no gifts under the tree. Many times, there was no tree. I saw birthdays passing unnoticed and school activities missed due to no available funds to attend.

"I witnessed the ridicule inflicted upon your mom and you kids by extended family, aunts, uncles, cousins, in-laws, teachers, counselors, business people, rent collectors, and fellow residents from places you had lived... and many others. Your mom became more and more reclusive — a social pariah.

"Any kindness shown to you and your family was a rare thing.

"When you were five or six, I saw the only time your father had done anything normal with his family. He took you kids to the Southeastern Fair in Atlanta.

"In fact, he abandoned you for good the same year when you were living in the garage apartment behind your landlady, Ruby's house on Center Hill Avenue. It was a long block away from Center Hill Elementary school.

"I saw the picture of you four taken during the trip to the fair with your dad. In the picture, from left to right there was David, you, Lynne, and Tim. Tim is the youngest. Your sister, Lynne is next in age, followed by you. David is the oldest.

"Do you recall this? There was something different or unique about each of you in this photo. Can you tell me what it was?" Jon said.

I answered, "Sure. I assume you mean beyond the fact later on Lynn and Tim had found the photo in mom's closet in the Capitol Homes, deciding to deface each of us by taking a needle coated with dabs of red colored medicine on its tip and poking holes in each of our eyes.

"Afterwards, we looked demonic with red holes for eyes. All four of us hated and loved the picture at the same time.

"Well, the unique thing about the photo was each of us had something we were holding or wearing we'd gotten at the fair. David was holding a golf ball he had found there. I was wearing a Hawaiian Lei made of plastic around my neck. It was placed there by one of the hoochie-coochie girls, working the crowd. Lynn had a windup furry cat attached to a stick the old man had won for her. Tim was crying, and he had soaked his pants by urinating in his blue jeans."

Jon jumped in, "I know you think Tim had the worst time of all of you. He was the youngest when all of this was happening, and in his life, he has suffered the most as a result of it. Your heart has always bled for Tim and Lynn. David and you were older and you could cope much better. But you two simply acted out differently, in a more positive 'kick-a-bush-instead' way."

"Does this answer your question, Jon?" I interrupted.

"Yes, it does. Great job. But hold on. There's always a big but with me. Can you tell me two other things? Why was Tim crying, and what made him wet his pants?" Jon stated.

Finally, he had me. After a minute or two of thought, I said, "Nope, you have got me there."

"Hah! All these years, Lynn and you have thought Tim was crying because he did not have anything to hold in the picture. This is incorrect. He was crying because he'd heard you and David screaming as you rode the Bullet Ride with your dad, and he was scared. So, he cried and wet his pants because your dad lifted him off the ground and gave him a forceful slap to the bottom for crying... once you three had exited the ride.

"Then, after the photo was taken, your dad gave Tim a quarter to get him to stop whimpering after threats to spank him again only brought louder crying. He took you home directly after this. He refused to learn how to be a parent," Jon replied.

Jon added, "I also saw the first day your family, minus Harold, moved into a garage apartment on Center Hill Street. I saw you trying to play tough the first day. A few of the neighborhood boys about your age taunted you, daring you to call an older girl an Indian name, 'Pocahontas.' They'd pointed her out to you as she walked towards the elementary school.

"You knew if you didn't comply a fight would ensue, and you'd be called a chicken forever. Fists would surely fly. You complied. You did this from a block away while she walked down your street, two blocks from the school. I saw she was wearing a long straight skirt, and she had silky black hair to her waist and dark skin.

"She heard you repeat the taunt louder and louder each time. It was like you were bragging now to new friends. Finally, she had heard enough. She screamed in your direction, 'You little brat.' Then, Pocahontas lifted her skirt above her knees so she could run faster. Darting towards you, she screamed threats to you.

"To you, she looked like a high school girl. At this opening, in Eric Carman style, you took off, running towards the school, huffing and puffing. Easily, she caught you, knocking you to the ground. Straddling you just beneath your shoulders, she made you apologize profusely, demanding you eat dirt several times. The playground consisted mostly of gravel.

"You complied fully without crying. All of the new boys laughed, watching from a safe distance on the playground. She looked around and threw a handful of gravel at them. Feigning a move towards the bunch, they scurried in all directions like the roaches do on the Capitol Homes floors in the hundreds when a light is switched on at night. This attractive girl was fast, strong, and feared.

"She picked you up, helped dust you off, and commented, 'Don't let those idiots get you in trouble again. They are no good. I watched you from my house while you moved in today. You didn't even cry, and believe me, each of them did when they got theirs. You're pretty brave. See you later, kid.'

"She walked away.

"The first day of the next school year you saw her at Center Hill Elementary. She was in the seventh grade. During lunch, when everyone was around, she walked up to you and kissed you on the cheek. She said, 'How are doing, Rod?' I saw your face turn as red as a pickled beet.

"She had helped you at Center Hill Elementary this day more than you have ever known. Rod, did you wonder why you never had to fight at the school for the two or so years you went there? Yep, Pocahontas was the reason.

"I watched two events when you lived in another government complex, the Ashby Street apartments.

"The first and saddest, occurred when you were four or five years old. There was a young girl your age, a neighbor, who lived in the apartment directly across from yours. In fact, the two apartments shared the same open porch and stairway to the sidewalk. You really liked the little girl whose name as I recall was Sally.

"I saw the day she came over to your apartment and invited David to her birthday party with a little formal invitation in his name. She was wearing a pretty pink dress. It was probably new and the clothes she was to wear for the evening party after supper was finished.

"She advised you were not invited and could not come. As she turned to exit the apartment, she hesitated when she reached the doorway. The door was wide open, and you told her, 'Go home now.'

"You were mad and seconds away from tears. The doors in those government apartments were big, thick, and heavy. You were unaware Sally had turned back to stick her tongue out at you. You were now behind the heavy door and closing it. You slammed the door shut to screams of pain from Sally.

"Inadvertently, she had placed her left hand in the crack between the door and door jam. As she leaned back in to taunt you further, instantly, three of her four fingers were completely severed. The little finger was hanging attached by skin only. Her thumb remained undamaged. Everyone from both apartments heard the screams and commotion and raced to the porch.

"Briefly, you stood there in the doorway in shock and crying. As everyone gathered, in tears, you kept repeating, 'I didn't mean to. I'm sorry. I'm sorry. I didn't mean to.'

"She was picked up by her father and carried into their apartment. Someone in the crowd shouted, 'Get some ice... put the fingers on ice.' Thankfully, this task was done quickly, and her parents exited the apartment in less than a minute, heading to Grady Hospital with her in their arms. Her hand was wrapped, and her detached fingers were in a big cup of ice.

"Some days later, I saw her arriving back home with her hand and arm heavily bandaged to her elbow. Shortly thereafter, they moved away. Rod, I can tell you over time she regained most of the usage of her reattached fingers. She led a normal life.

"The second event I witnessed from the same apartment complex was after a horrible rain and electric storm had occurred.

"Your family had thought you were killed — washed away by the day's torrential rains.

"You and brother David had walked up to Sears in West End just before the storm hit. You'd remained inside the store, knocking about, trying to wait the storm out before heading back home.

"It was getting late. In the pouring rain, you exited the store to hurry home. You lagged behind David. He left you farther and farther behind. David made it to the steps of your apartment and looked back for you. You were nowhere in sight. He decided he better backtrack and find you so as not to upset your mom. He could not find you. He was able to locate one of your pink flip flops floating at the top of a drainage site at the side of the road-way. David tried his best to find you there in the flooded hole.

"Did you know he actually got in the hole and came close to drowning himself, searching for you? The current was too strong even for David. He held onto the cement above water level for dear life as he submerged his head underwater trying to find you or your lifeless little body — and yes, Rod, tell Jim and your other two friends you were small and thinner back then.

"David ran home screaming with your flip flop in hand as evidence you were gone, washed away, and he had tried to save you.

"All your relatives and the Atlanta Police were called by the use of a neighbor's phone. Nanny and Papa were first to arrive, followed by the police and your mother's two sisters. Uncle Fred arrived last.

"Your Ashby Street apartment was filled with people eager to start a search for you. The police began to coordinate the effort, assigning where each person or team would search.

"At this point, your aunt Hazel spotted you hiding behind the couch against the wall, whimpering softly. She stood up, quieted everyone, and said, 'Rod is behind the couch.' You could see her pointing down at you. Your mom snatched you from there and plopped you on the top of the heat radiator.

"Everyone in the room watched as your mom sat you on the radiator in the living room and paddled your naked rump.

"It seemed you were completely nude behind the couch. You'd slipped into the house when David and your mom first went out-side... down the street a bit looking for you. Before people started to arrive at your apartment, you had time to undress and hide naked behind the couch.

"You have not been more embarrassed since. I can also affirm the radiator was hot. They tended to be year round back then in the few housing projects in Atlanta.

"Next, I saw you and David, your older brother, fighting a lot every place you moved and at every new school you attended.

"David became your hero, father figure, and brother in one. He was the person you wanted to be like. 'Be like David' was your motto and your mantra in those years.

"I saw your younger brother in and out of juvenile. I saw your grandparents, mom, and you in tow most times getting him out of juvenile.

"I saw all the odd jobs you worked as a youth and all the money you spent on your sister, younger brother, and mom for clothes, food, and cigarettes. You started working at six and by the time you were eight years old, you held several odd jobs at the same time. You were moonlighting as a child.

"Your mother was well-loved but actually pitied by you and your siblings. Alone, in those days, she was incapable of providing for you. She smoked heavily three to four packs a day, and naturally, smoking was an expense and habit your family didn't need.

"Without Nanny and Papa, Welfare, the Federal Free Food Program, the State of Georgia, public health clinics, and doctors doing voluntary work for the poor, you would not have made it.

"As you would expect, your older brother became the male head of the household at the tender age of eight. Like many others, your mother adored David.

"I watched David as a sixteen-year-old having a verbal fight in the Capitol Homes with your mother. It had turned physical. Ultimately, he shoved her down onto the cement floor where she broke her arm. He stormed out this summer night, and he never returned to her or his siblings for the rest of his life. It was due

to a girl and a phone call. To this day, deep-rooted tensions exist
between you four siblings.

"You moved around a lot, attending nine or ten different elementary schools. At one of these, you were well-received and
treated. It was one year in the fourth grade when you lived briefly with your maternal grandparents, Nanny and Papa. Mrs.
Wilkins was a kind and warm-hearted teacher who changed
your academic life for the better.

"Your mentor and only positive male role model in your life
was your Papa, John Quincy Walker. He was like a rock for
you. He was a great man and not even blood related to you.
He was your mother's stepfather and thus your step grandfather.
Your family lost him in 1968 after a long debilitating battle with
lung cancer. A year or so before this time, you had also left
home, following David to live with your maternal grandparents.

"I saw your mother marry a young ex-convict who ran your
younger brother, Tim, and sister, Lynn, from their Capitol Homes
apartment. Mostly, they slept on park benches and on occasion,
with friends. They lived homeless for weeks. I saw you trying to
find them in the Capitol Homes area to make them come home
with you to Nanny's and Papa's.

"I saw your stepfather shoot your mother in the arm through
a door with a twenty-two caliber rifle. He was trying to kill her.
She survived.

"Your Nanny, Effie Vera Walker, was like a mother to you and
your siblings.

"For you five, life was tougher than even I could've imagined.
The hunger, losses of water, electricity for lights, and gas for heat
and cooking were frequent. Eventually, your younger brother
and sister were legally taken over by your grandmother. They
were forced into this, and their lives spiraled down from here.

"I saw you and David excel in sports and academics in
elementary and high school. You both became co-presidents
of your high school's student body.

"I saw David and you receive scholarships and student loans to attend college at Mercer University. Both of you worked hard during the school year and summers to help pay your college costs.

"I watched David turn his back on you at Mercer to the point many of your same fraternity brothers didn't know you and he were blood brothers. It was apparent David wanted it this way then as well as to this day. Like your father, he left all of you, but at the time, David was a teenager or a young man. You've always been proud he was your big brother, and I saw you'd forgiven him.

"I witnessed you attain a BA from Georgia State University in English Literature in 1974 while working fulltime as a rookie policeman in Atlanta. I saw David earn a BS in Economics at Mercer University two years earlier.

"I saw David as he moved to Colorado where he lives today.

"I watched you and Rose marry in 1973 and the birth of your daughter, Faye, in 1980. The love and dedication you and Rose have for her is overwhelming. I saw the baby Rose and you had lost before Faye was born.

"I saw you become an Atlanta police officer in the spring of 1973. Over the years, you rose through the ranks to Captain. I saw everything which occurred with you in your profession. I saw all the close calls, the good deeds, the people whose lives you saved, and the tragedies, including the ultimate one involving the shoot-ing death of your nephew while on duty with the Atlanta Police Department. I know to this day you blame yourself. He wanted to follow in your career. Rose and you pleaded with him not to join the force. She felt he was too small and would get hurt. You knew where his heart was, and regardless of what you said, he was going to join. It's not your fault.

"I saw how the event devastated your sister, Lynn, and her husband, Walter. He was their oldest son.

"So, here we are now. You've led a colorful life," he stated.

A Colorful Life

"I have led a colorful life? Let me tell you a little about this life which was mostly void of any color. Jon, I cannot recall one indelible moment of real happiness either of my parents experienced. Mom was chronically sad her entire life. Do not misunderstand me. There were times of joy, laughter, and some moments of hope, but they were always experienced with guilt and a misperception we weren't worthy of such emotions. Every minute and everything seemed dire to us. It sounds silly to describe it in this manner, but even the urgency of our human condition became dreadfully urgent. Hunger will cause these feelings.

"We lived daily in the posttraumatic stress of yesterday combined with the added futility of tomorrow. The actual 'today' was the worst. Mom had all the pressure. I know for a fact she punished herself by the minute for her failures — failure at being a wife, at keeping a husband, being a mother, a provider, an educator, a mentor, and most of all, failure at not knowing how to be both father and mother, gatherer, and nurturer. Her daily life was a dismal reminder of all she could not do. In our lives, there was no yin to the our yang, no light to the dark, or no positive opposing the negative. My siblings and I lived on the edge of mom's thousand-yard stare. I tried my best to get closer. At times, it felt like I was closing the distance, but she was too far gone. Comatose would be too harsh of a description for mom but functioning minimally while hypnotized would not be. She had a hard life.

"In his novel *A Tale of Two Cities,* Charles Dickens had it right, *'It was the best of times, it was the worst of times.'*

"Jon, the day she died, my mom thought my dad would return to her and us. He had been gone from us for over 21 years. Mom suffered an agonizing, prolonged, and miserable death. She didn't deserve this disease. If any child of God deserved better, mom was one. He did take the pain away. She always said she was in no pain. A cancer ate away at her face, eye, skull, and brain. After I had visited her, while in police uniform, I can't advise you the number of times I wanted to end her misery and suffering. I had the means. There was no one there to comfort her or a son to say a final time, 'I love you, little Momsie.' In a nursing home, she died alone and bedridden of cancer. Her disease was horrific, rare, and inoperable.

"Looking back, it is somewhat sad to acknowledge the years we lived in the Capitol Homes were the best ones of our lives or at least they were for my brothers, my sister, and me.

"Jon, consider this scenario of life as a young boy. What if you had traveled back to the farm, and you had no responsibilities unless you chose to have them? There was no parental authority and at most, a minimum of adult control over you. You had no rules, no set bedtime, and no set anything. There was no parental demand you go to school, but if you did, there were no expectations of success. You had no conscience, no respect for others or their property, and worst of all, no respect for yourself. You had plenty of friends and foes in the same circumstances. There were no authority figures beyond the long arm of the law and no lack of family... if you chose the right gang to run with. There was no religion, no church, and beyond those you set on yourself, there were no boundaries. If these things applied to you, how would your life have been?

"Jon, before you answer, I have a few conditions and consequences to consider. You will need to know these to make an informed decision. With the entire package above and more, you still have the small print. Day by day, the package may seem to be, or actually be, wonderful, but those days grow short with lifelong consequences — if you actually live a long life. Many die young due to the 'life' I described. There are a ton of considerations or conditions which apply like drugs, alcohol, jails, detention beatings, police adjusting your attitude, guns, gang fights, knives, lead pipes, crimes to commit, people to rob, cars to jack, homes to burgle, boxcars to empty, animals and peers to torture, things to burn, property to steal, hustling to do, sex to sell and buy, drug and booze addiction, murder (a reality as victim or perpetrator), and worst of all, no proper education, and no meaningful future. Many of these are there before you make it to high school age.

"Jon, allow me answer the question for you. The next time we're called up, thank the Man for the life you have lived. Surely, He has seen both of ours.

"Like any other jungle, the projects could swallow you whole at any time. There was potential harm on every block and on the congested streets. Real citizens, passing through in cars, loved to put us in their rearview mirrors as quickly as possible — unless of course, the men were there to pick up young boys.

"Living in the Capitol Homes, was like camping on the shoulder of any Interstate Highway. They should have placed signs stating 'No Pedestrians Allowed' throughout the area. A pedestrian lifestyle is the exact opposite of life in the shadows of the Georgia State Capitol. The only gold in this area covered the building's dome. Poverty will turn anyone into a gold miner, looking for anything free which sparkles... while having nothing.

"It was a tough life in the projects. It had to be rougher on the adults. The children received no break. We all suffered. It was only a matter of context or how much each family could endure.

"On any given evening, we could tell you what each household was having for dinner. We 'patrolled' the homes like a ravenous pack of rats. The air was filled with the fragrances of 'bean de jour.' On this particular example or evening within my memory, my nose said we were having butter beans, the Smiths were downing pinto beans, the Burtons were eating navy beans, the, Bells were sipping cabbage soup again, and the Russells, who had a father at home, were having a breakfast supper with bacon. Except for the Russells, everyone else was also having cornbread and sweetened iced tea.

"So much for the best years of our lives."

Suddenly, I did not feel so colorful, and Jonathan saw it in me.

Excitedly, Jon sprang from the bench and said, "I discovered something yesterday when you entered the tree. This was the first time I had ushered anyone into the tree. But when I went back to the bench and looked up at the tree, I saw you or your colors bouncing from limb to limb, branch to branch, up and down, and left and right all the way to the top. At times, it was like lights twinkling on and off all over the tree, and at other times, it was like slow motion photography, showing streaming street traffic and lights all over a busy city at night. When you reached the top, a solid rainbow-colored light shot into the heavens. It was a wide beam of bright lights.

"Watch, I'll show you." He darted under the tree and looked up. Instantly, the light show started. It was a kaleidoscope of colors and shapes as he moved all about the tree. Before he made it to the top, the tree was filled with colors like an over lit Christmas tree. It was glorious... absolutely stunning. Next, the top lights shot skyward with no end in sight. There was movement within this thick circular beam, streaming to the heavens.

"Boy, can Jonathan bring the color back or what!" I thought.

To Love Is to Be Happy With

I sat there, watching the tree and its top explode in 3D color and HD clarity throughout its body to the tip of its top, while his being traveled at light speed or better towards the heavens. As he returned, the topper beam seemed to collapse from the heavens down into the tree. As quickly as he had left, he was back in his body, standing beneath the limbs. Smiling wild-eyed at me like a young boy, Jon stood there for a few seconds before joining me on our bench.

"It's time to tell me a little about the guys," he demanded.

"Before I do, will you tell me one thing?" I responded.

"Sure, ask away," he replied.

"Let me preface this a little. If you feel uncomfortable and do not want to discuss it, I'll fully understand, seriously. I'd really like to hear about your wife and child, but if the pain is too great, we can change the subject," I stated.

"Her name is Lucy, and she lives as surely as all of our loved ones do.

"Lucy and I had known each other for many years. She was five years younger than I. Her family lived on the closest farm to ours. It was about ten miles to the north of us and nestled within eyesight of the Hudson River.

"As you can imagine, during this period, we settlers tried as best we could to band together in the good times and in the bad ones.

"There were three main tribes of Indians who lived in the general region. Two of them were peaceful in nature, causing no problems, but the third was anything but friendly. Most of the time, the three fought amongst themselves for various reasons usually centered on hunting areas, access to water, or land rights.

"The few farmers up and down the Hudson made it a point to protect each other as much as humanly possible.

"The winter of 1558 was harsh. Hunting was bad, and folks, native and settler alike, were suffering. But as always, we banded together, helping each other during this winter.

"The Harnish family owned the outermost parcel of flatland about twenty miles northeast of the Smiths, Lucy's family. The Harnish family was attacked first. The Smiths would be next.

"My dad and I made the ten miles to Lucy's home in a blistering snow storm to gather them up to be brought back to our farm for safety. In such times, safety in numbers was prudent against any further attacks by the natives. Ours was the best fortified farm with well-built structures for protection and defense. There were only three of us and plenty of room for neighbors in harm's way.

"Mom stayed behind with my Uncle Pete who was visiting his sister this winter from the southern wilderness, which in part is now Georgia. Pete could play a banjo like no other, but he had learned to love the moonshine. My mom frowned on his drinking. On occasion, dad also enjoyed a snort or two. I was never a drinker or smoker. Uncle Pete could tell some whoppers about the southern frontier.

"Lucy, her two brothers, her mom, and dad gathered up all the necessities for a prolonged stay. They brought their two horses, a mule, and their milking cow for the trip to our farm. During the unrest of the winter, they stayed with us just over three weeks.

"No other farms were attacked and no other settlers harmed.

"The Harnishs were lucky to escape the attack with only minor wounds and injuries, but they lost all of their livestock and food reserves. After the assault, they stayed at the Butler farm below ours.

"It had been a few years since I had really paid any notice to Lucy, but for some reason, this time she was different. She had matured into a graceful young lady. She was stunning. Lucy was always intelligent and funny when it was needed. Mainly, she communicated with her smiles and facial expressions. She was a quiet and proper lady.

"In the evenings, we would take turns reading verses from the good book to our guests. These words were soothing, especially in this time of uncertainty.

"I was instantly smitten. Oddly, a few years earlier, mom had told me she'd seen in a dream Lucy was for me, and she would be my wife. It embarrassed the life out of me. It is strange how some dreams can come true.

"Like I said, I was hopelessly in love. Lucy wasn't. I tried to spend as many minutes and hours I could with her during the three week period.

"You might not believe this, but she was just as beautiful back then as any woman I've seen since. She had silky blonde hair, falling down to her thin waist. She had a most pleasing build and grayish-blue eyes — more gray than blue but two-toned still. Lucy's skin was as soft and white as a fresh bar or lye soap or a glass of cow's milk. She smelled of lilacs. Lucy stood about 5' 7" which was rather tall back then for women. As you can see, I'm only about an inch taller. She could stand toe to toe with me and stare at me eye to eye.

"She was a force to be reckoned with. Both mom and dad loved it and her. They saw I was a dead duck. It was in every glance I made her way. Slowly, I chipped away at her defenses, and by the end of three weeks, we were holding hands and taking long walks in the snow. The cold didn't seem to bother us.

"In the first month of the next spring, I kissed her down by the Hudson during a multi-family get together and asked her parents for her hand. Lucy was asked third after her parents and mine.

"We were wed in the spring on the bank of the Hudson River not one hundred yards from this tree and land. We had plans before the end of the coming summer to build our own cabin closer to the river on the far end of dad's land.

"I've always loved rivers.

"In the meantime, we lived in my parents' home. Mom and dad adored Lucy, and officially, with announcement, she became their daughter, seeing how they had none.

"Within a few months, Lucy and I were going to be parents. So, we postponed the cabin construction for the moment. Mom insisted on this. Lucy carried our child in the womb for six months. One Saturday morning, while milking our cow, Lucy was kicked in the stomach by the cow. The cow was spooked by a rat as it darted between her front hoofs.

"The cow wasn't to blame, neither was the rat, but Lucy went straight into labor. My son, Patrick, was born dead. None of us could stop the bleeding. There was not a doctor within a seventy mile radius of the farm.

"Lucy passed quietly, holding our son cradled in her right arm. I held her left hand wrapped in both of mine. Mom, dad, and I wept openly.

"We buried mother and child together in the Huna family plot between the farm and Hudson River.

"I trust you can understand my burning desire to join them as soon as possible. I've waited over four hundred and fifty years," he stated in tears.

In silence, we sat for a short period. Jon fought his tears and sadness like most men will do when they come. Within a few minutes, he was looking much better... more like his usual self.

"Jon, I am so sorry about your loss of Lucy, Patrick, your mom, and dad, but you will be with them again sooner than you think. I hope," I said.

I added, "Although, I really don't look forward to your departure. I've grown used to our chats, and Lord knows, I could use more of your help.

"Your greatly extended life sounds fascinating. In fact, it would have to be since no one else in the verifiable recorded history of man has lived so long. You should have written books about it. What am I saying, you may well have.

"Jon, please tell me more. I would like nothing better than to hear about your life from the beginning. There are plenty of questions I'd like to ask you, but I am eager to hear more about you and your family.

"The first question I'd like answered is a doozy. In all the years since the death of Lucy and in all the places you have traveled, did you remarry and have a family?"

Slowly, Jon began. "Rod, since I lost Lucy, I have never remarried. You see, mainly by our mothers, Lucy and I were schooled at home in all the pertinent subjects of the time. We had Bible studies, religions, philosophy, and literature. Mainly, our curriculums consisted of reading, writing, and arithmetic but with a lot of history and proper etiquette thrown in.

"There were times when we had a traveling preacher to come up the Hudson on a flatboat with a small wooden cabin or hut built on it. Preacher would travel the Hudson spreading the gospel from his floating chapel about once every two or three months, weather permitting. When he docked near the surrounding settlements, we would come from miles just to hear him. He would usually stay three or four days at each stop up and down the river.

"In our general area, the few settlers would gather by the river and listen to his sermons. We were often there for two or three days of his messages. He would baptize those who were ready to accept Jesus as their savior and bless the newborn babies, if there were any. I can only remember six, maybe eight, newborns to be blessed. His name was Preacher Ray.

"I never knew if this was his family name or given name, but he was always simply Preacher Ray. He presided over our spring wedding there next to the Hudson. For the most part, Preacher Ray lived on what those who received his messages would give. Along his journey up and down the river three times a year in favorable weather, he'd accept the offerings. During the long harsh winters, there'd be no formal worshiping to be had, but the good book was always book one in our house and Lucy's.

"After Lucy died, there was no other woman for me. Call me old fashioned if you will. The 'until death we do part' oath meant forever and unto eternity to me, and I knew Lucy felt the same. Nah, Lucy was the one for me. I am far too old to set up housekeeping again."

"Tell me a little about your youth? You obviously know most of mine from what you have already divulged about it, so, quid pro quo, dude, quid pro quo," I stated.

Jonathan laughed at this.

Suddenly, I realized how much I liked the sound of the name Jonathan. It was a strong name and in respect to Jon, a pious one. At this point, he was the perfect embodiment of the meek who will inherit the Earth. Jon was a meek man who looked thirty and in many ways, acted ancient. It was obvious at this time he was weary from all the years, and death looked awfully comforting to him. After all, he knew where he would soon be.

Jon smiled childishly and said, "Oh, yes, the pastoral and idyllic farm life.

"The earliest age I can remember anything from is around three. I can recall being terrified of our chickens and the roosters. Whenever I got near them, they used to peck me.

"There were days when dad would allow the chickens to roam freely on the grounds around the house and within the split rail fencing surrounding our farmhouse and out buildings. I later learned this was done to police or clean the area. The chickens and roosters would peck away and clean any errant kernels of corn or other droppings from the ducks and geese, frequenting the inner grounds.

"Birds can be nasty creatures.

"Well, as I said, they almost scared me to death. I would cry and run for mom's skirt tail every time they were near. She started me out slowly, making me feed the chickens a bit from the outside of their pen while they were inside theirs. She would carry me to the barn, and I would get both hands full of cracked corn. Mom would then lead me over to the pen, and I would toss the corn inside to the chickens.

"After a short time, this became fun for me, and I would laugh at the chickens like crazy. Then, mom would start laughing at me, and dad, when he was there, if he was not out in the fields or doing a million other things around the farm at the time, would be laughing like crazy too at me and mom. This became my first real chore at the age of three. Soon, I had the responsibility of feeding the chickens every day at the same time.

"Then, mom showed me other fun things to do during the day. By the time I was four or five, I was feeding the chickens, making sure the firewood, and kindling were brought in by the fire three times a day, before dawn, midday, and after supper at dusk.

"Next, all day, I was to keep the fresh water coming from the well. We had an excellent, deep, and bountiful well. The water was cold and sweet, almost as if there were a kiss of honey in each ladle. Rod, no kidding, it was delicious.

"She had dad make me a small hoe, and I was taught how to rid the rows of weeds in the family vegetable and herb gardens next to the house. Then, it totally became one of my chores.

"It was a rather large garden for an inside the yard area one. Our yard was of dirt and small pebble rocks. When I grew older, mom and I would rake the rocks into patterns in the yard for Sunday. It was our lawn work of the time.

"We had a nice outhouse — rather close to the chicken coop but just far enough away from the house. During windy winter months, near the Hudson, you learned how to hold it at night or almost freeze to death, trekking to the privy from your bed. We kept a pot under our beds for those chilly emergencies. It was a rather comfy two-seater, and before long, its cleanliness became my responsibility. It was a dirty chore similar to keeping the stalls of the barn cleaned — another of my chores.

"On the farm, everything had value. We used most waste as fertilizer. We wasted nothing usable.

"In the summer garden, we had tomatoes of several varieties, okra, yellow crookneck squash, zucchini, bell peppers, red chili peppers, pole beans, purple hull peas, cucumbers, and a section of herbs. The peppers were planted far away from the other flowering vegetables or else everything would taste like them.

"In the fields, outside the fence, primarily, we grew corn during the summer, but we also had root plants such as peanuts, potatoes, beets, carrots, collard greens, and mustard greens. We grew pumpkins, watermelons, cantaloupes, grapes, and scuppernongs. We had quite an orchard too with fig, apple, peach, pear, and cherry trees. During the fall, we grew fall crops and summer, summer crops.

"Then, there were the off-season cover crops, Indian corn to grind for feed, and hay to cut, gather, bundle, stack, and store for the animals.

"At age six, my chores had grown exponentially. Like dad and mom, I worked from before sunup to after sundown, and I had classes daily after meals.

"We had a couple of wagons, one for traveling with buckboard seats for the family, and one more for work, hauling things around the farm and to the local gatherings where crops were bartered from season to season each year.

"We had chickens, layers, red and bantam roosters, pullets, and bantams. We had hogs, two mules, dad's riding horse, two milk cows, a few head of cattle for meat when the deer hunting was scarce, a pet cat named Kitten, and a couple of beagle hunting dogs named Ricky and Tiny. Our dogs loved mom like she had given birth to them. Kitten was her pick.

"I used to maintain a few pigeon nests in the rafters inside the roof of the barn for squab and fresh pigeon eggs. Dad and I loved piping hot cathead biscuits, pan-fried squab, and scrambled pigeon eggs on wintery mornings. Mom wouldn't eat the tiny birds or the pigeon eggs, but on request, she'd cook them just the same for us.

"In those days, the available wildlife for food was plentiful. We had fish, frogs, turtles, venison, squirrels, doves, quails, and rabbits to catch or hunt. If things were really dire during winter, we'd resort to hunting raccoon and opossum for food.

"We always had to prepare for winter, and the wind howled like banshees in all directions or it seemed like it did. A solid eight months of the year, we were preparing for the first snows of fall. Winter always hit us like a hammer. We stockpiled wood, smoked and cured meats and fish, and mason jars of preserves of everything possible from the farm.

"The winters were harshest on the livestock. We had a large barn with a hay loft, housing all of our livestock. The hogs could come inside the barn into their own penned in area near the back of the barn. The chickens had their wooden shack or coup close to the structure.

"We had a small smokehouse and storage house. We also had a small ice house. It had thick walls sealed and insulated with thin sheets of hammered copper which cost dad a summer's crop of available corn in trade. But boy, we loved the ice during the summer months. Originally, mom had wanted the icehouse, and dad jumped on it.

"Each year, we harvested blocks of ice from frozen spring-fed ponds, small lakes in the area. Sometimes, we bartered for blocks of ice which were delivered down the river from the north each year on large barges on their way south toward more populated areas. A house full of block ice would last us almost into the next winter."

I interrupted, "Jon, I have to tell you this. Back in the early 2000s, Rose, Faye, and I stayed in a custom-built house in New Orleans. It was constructed from old large planks of wood taken from ice barges like you described. The house was in a fenced compound, and it had an old ice house which was converted into an apartment on the grounds. The owner told us a graduate student in engineering had received a federal grant to build the two units from the historical wood of ice barges and materials from an old New Orleans ice house. The compound was fascinating. The dark wood used in the house's construction was thick, wide, and heavy. We loved this vacation. Sorry, please continue."

"No problem. It was interesting. If we had the time, it would be great to visit it. I would love to see it," Jon said.

He continued, "Where was I? Oh, there was a root cellar off the rear of the house where we stored our preserved goods and root products. When necessary, we used it as a storm cellar.

"Our house was made of sturdy logs from trees with ample clay and cut straw cement insulation inside and out. The house had two doors and five fortified windows with storm shudders on them for protection.

"There was a large open fireplace for all the cooking and a pot belly stove we kept fired up during the winter months for more heat.

"Mom made most of our clothes, and we wore them as long as possible. She made house rags from them. Nothing went to waste.

"Dad and I slaughtered a hog every season when the cold weather got just right. The whole process took about a week to complete. For the following season, we consumed everything but the bones and oink from our winter hog.

"What we did not have but needed, we would barter for with our few neighbors. We had plenty of corn and other vegetables to trade.

"Mr. Harnish grew tobacco as his barter crop. Dad loved to smoke a bowl in his clay pipe in the evening after supper and sundown. Mom disliked the smell. She'd make him sit real close to the big fire, directing his exhaled smoke up the chimney. Our fireplace was built properly, and it had a strong draw.

"Dad was a master at everything. He could fix anything, and he was as smart as a whip. He and mom had an ease and calmness together. To this day, it warms my heart.

"Before long, by about age seven, I was tasked with selecting the fryer for each Sunday's big meal. We always had fried chicken on Sunday's — always. We had chickens like a rabbit farmer raises bunnies. Lucy used to love to kid us about it. Lucy would joke almost every Sunday morning, 'Mom, Jon and I have agreed, we would like fried chicken today.'

"When I was younger, I never considered where the meat we ate came from. Back then, mom and dad kept these things away from me. By age seven, I was picking the chicken, ringing its neck by hand, plucking is feathers, and gutting it for the Sunday table. Mom always sectioned and fried it. Dad would serve it.

"Our farmhouse had three rooms. The house's main big room was the initial log cabin dad and mom built when they first settled here. Later, dad added two bedrooms and a front and back porch to it. It was a big house for three. The settlers always pitched in for new arrivals, helping build their first house. It was a joyous occasion for all.

"One nice spring Sunday, I was sitting under one of the main room windows, plucking a chicken, when I overheard mom and dad talking. Mom was quietly crying. Dad was trying to console her. I was about ten at this time. I overheard mom was sad because it was the anniversary of the last child she had lost. During this, it was revealed I was actually the third child for mom and dad. Mom had lost two children to miscarriages within three years before I was born. I never knew this. Folks held things real close to their vests those days. They were proud and secure people, willing to always help others but never asking for it themselves. This is exactly how people were back then. Refreshing, isn't it?

"My mom was perfect. She worked harder than me and dad combined. She never complained except about dad's pipe smoke. She would cut her eyes in his direction when he took more than one or two slugs from the chilled Apple Jack jug.

"She was always the first up and the last to bed. Every evening, she would see me to bed, kiss dad goodnight, and he was off to their bed. Dad and I would be out like a lit candle in a strong gust of wind. In seconds, he would be snoring like one of the hogs. Mom would continue working until all her chores were done, and after the candles were blown out, she was off to join dad.

"We were true believers of the 'early to bed, early to rise' thing penned by Ben Franklin some two hundred years later. Mom was the cement which held us together. They were loving parents. I cannot recall a day in my thirty years at home I was not told by both I was loved... not one day.

"I liked hunting and fishing. As a teenager, those chores became my favorites. But I could not spend too much time in the woods or on the river because my other chores had to be kept up.

"Several times a year, usually during planting or harvesting times, the settlers up and down the valley would gather at one of the farms and have a big get together, lasting about three days or so. It was a time of games, dancing, music, singing, eating, races, trading, storytelling, spooky tales, and courting and sparking for some of the single young adults there. More than a few new unions began at those gatherings.

"From year to year, Lucy was always there as were a few other young girls and boys. She would flirt somewhat with one of the Peterson boys from across the river. This usually got in my craw. Mom would spot it on my face in a second and nudge me to go over there and fight for her. Mom knew I fancied her, and she also knew Lucy liked me much more than the Peterson boy.

"I was always too shy even though I was five years her senior. At the time, I was a seasoned teenager who didn't know squat about women. I had too many chores to do to worry about such folly. Nevertheless, I'd make sure to get at least one dance with her at every gathering simply to annoy the Peterson boy. During one of our dances, I caught Lucy as she stuck her tongue out at him. I laughed and told mom later in the evening. She simply said, 'Told you.' She smiled and walked off.

"Dad could usually be found enjoying a snort or two with the men as they smoked their cigars, rolled cigarettes, and various types of pipes. A few of them chewed or sniffed their tobacco.

"One night, I overheard them talking, and basically, it revolved around saving the world from the French trappers and English gentry, roaming our domains more and more often.

"During these gatherings, some natives from the two peaceful tribes of Indians in the area would attend. Those young boys were tough. They could play sports, and the girls were beautiful with shiny black hair and dark features. Oddly, those long-haired girls reminded me of my mom. If she'd had long hair, she could have easily passed as the mother of any of the pretty Indian girls.

"The next thirteen years or so came and went. Life on the farm was all I knew. Day and night, we three stayed busy. In those days survival wasn't a guarantee. You had to work as hard and as long as you could to keep your nose above water.

"The hostility of the bad tribe was growing every year. Mainly, they remained on the other side of the river. The Petersons and others on their side of the Hudson caught hell. The Peterson boy Lucy flirted with was killed during an attack on their farm. His mother was also critically wounded. Lucy and her mother traveled over and stayed with their family for weeks after the attack. Lucy helped nurse Mrs. Peterson back to health. I felt sorry for the Petersons and their son.

"Then, there came my wedding followed by Lucy and Patrick's deaths, my months of grieving, and lastly, the tree.

"At the age of eighty-six, my father died in the winter of 1599. He is buried in the family cemetery with mom, Lucy, and my son, Patrick.

"The following summer, my mother passed away at the age of eighty-one of heart failure. To this day, I believe her death was from a broken heart after losing the love of her life. She is buried beside father next to Lucy and Patrick.

"I attended both of their funerals from a distance. I remained long after the mourners had left. Until my mother's funeral, I had not known she was also five years younger than the love of her life.

"Over the centuries, I have visited them often. The cemetery has grown, but it has always been maintained with funds provided by an anonymous donor. If possible, I'd thank him and shake his hand.

"After my initial tree adventure and miracle, working each year as I was directed has been as hectic as any year on the farm. Like I have told you, I've traveled the world many times. Early on, this was no easy thing. I was directed by the voice every step of the way.

"Nothing bad ever happened to the tree or the land we see before us. No matter how long I was gone, it was there when I returned. I assumed it did not vanish when I traveled. But as far as I knew, it could have. After what had occurred with me because of the tree, this made as much sense as anything else.

"I wrote everywhere I went. I was told early on how important this new world was going to become, and it would succeed where many have failed. Always per order, I would volunteer and fight in every skirmish or war in which the new nation involved itself, and this was a hundred or more years before there was a new nation.

"Eventually, this new country came... growing slowly, and off I still went to all the different wars. I was always directed to remain an entry level soldier or grunt as we've been called in the past. I fought in most of them without as much as a scratch. A couple of times, the Vietnam and Iraq wars, I was in the rear with the gear. No Purple Hearts for me. As ordered, I flew below the radar and fought as a buck private.

"I fought in the Battle of New Orleans, the Spanish American War, the Revolutionary War, the Civil War, the American Indian War or uprisings in the west, World War I in France, World War II in the Pacific with the Marines. I also fought in the Korean War, Vietnam, Desert Storm, and Iraqi Freedom. I was spared the Afghanistan one.

"Like a ghost, impervious to pain or injury, I fought on, and I am certain I saved a number of lives of my fellow soldiers in the process. I am proudest of this. All the while, I traveled and I wrote in foxholes, ditches, and bunkers all over the world.

"The wonders I've seen at their inception from the mid 1560s to this date have been phenomenal. The future events had always been revealed and shown beforehand to me. This never negated their majesty.

"I saw this country spring from the wilderness settlements like we farmed before the Plymouth Rock arrival. I witnessed the Pilgrims arrive and almost starve and the French, Spanish, and English as they fought to control the territories later known as the United States. I saw the slaughter of General Custer who could easily have been Pops or Thomas who are a lot like him. Ego will always get you in the end.

"Rod, I saw the birth of a nation, swamp lands become Washington, DC, slavery, trains headed west, dams built, electricity run to family homes, first flight at Kitty Hawk, our space program, and assassinations of presidents and funerals. I witnessed fever and death, pestilence and polio, the explosion of the Hindenburg, building of skyscrapers, prohibition, flappers, speakeasies, gang warfare, organized crime, America growing, prospering, the cure for polio, the first man on the moon, Sputnik, the holocaust, nuclear testing, nuclear bombs dropped during WWII, righteous men assassinated, carpet bombing of Vietnam and Cambodia, the Wall go down, the Twin Towers falling, the screams of a nation, Detroit's destruction at the hands of corrupt politicians, and these past five years of gloom and doom in America where among Americans malaise and futility run as thick as molasses in December… and on and on.

"I have seen too much. My eyelids are like straight razors against my eyeballs. I am weak, and I am weary. I am tried, and I am ready to be with Lucy and Patrick.

"No, I never remarried, Rod," Jon sadly repeated.

Quiet consumed us.

Mercer and Friends

After a few minutes, I stated, "Before I get into those characters, let me tell you a little about Mercer University in Macon, Georgia where three members of my family studied.

"My older brother, David, was the first to head for Mercer. He was an excellent athlete. He was recruited by many major colleges to play football. He was great at all sports. His senior year of high school, he was injured while warming up for a football game. It was a serious injury. Seemingly, his sports career was over. David was highly recruited by Mercer to play baseball, and he had several friends from other area high schools who were Mercer students. They'd come over to our grandparent's house and try to talk David into coming to Mercer. He did, and within weeks, he was enamored with the whole Mercer Bears college scene.

"As a junior and senior in high school, I used to visit campus some. I had three other friends going there, due to David's recommendations. He was a member of the Kappa Sigma fraternity there. During his first two years in Macon, I attended a couple of their fraternity parties. After high school, I was Mercer bound and busy satisfying my motto — 'be like David.'

"Mercer was and is a wonderful university with first class educators. It is a private Liberal Arts university with Judeo-Christian religious affiliations. In the 1970s, the undergraduate school had around 2,000 students. It also had a Graduate School and Law

School with approximately 500 more students. You were definitely not just a number at Mercer U. The entire experience was personal. Most of the professors fostered a cooperative spirit. It was a pleasant student and faculty atmosphere.

"The student-friendly campus has a rustic, almost Ivy League, appearance and feel to it.

"Macon, GA has a colorful southern history. There is only one negative aspect of where Mercer is located. If the cloud cover and wind were just right, the aroma of paper mills would fill the air. Other than this, Macon is an exciting quaint city. Its central location is ideal for a day trip to Atlanta, a short weekend trip to Savannah, the Georgia Coast, or either coast of Florida. Macon also has a vibrant music, arts, and literary community.

"Many young women and men from wealthy families throughout the southeast attended Mercer. At the same time, Mercer had an aggressive scholarship, grants, and student aid program for the indigent applicant. David and I were fortunate to have been offered financial assistance and student loans to attend.

"Mercer's main emphasis was on academic excellence. In short, the school was tough. Back then, we had a university-sponsored program known as 'Wonderful Wednesday.' There were no classes or tests on Wednesday. You might think, 'Whoopee!' Not so fast there, boys and girls. The professors loved and hated the program. They loved it because they also were free to take Wonderful Wednesday off. They hated it because every week Tuesday became another weekend night, and they needed the extra day to teach. An additional night to blow a little steam off sounded excellent to us. The professors always tripled up on us on Tuesday with extra reading and writing assignments. We learned a valuable technique in this situation... how to cram without sleep.

"Life on the campus of Mercer University was as close to perfection as a young man or woman will find. As dire as things often seemed, we managed to have loads of fun and mentally go as far academically as we allowed ourselves to be taken by our professors.

"I cannot overstate the importance of being a person rather than a number. Mercer taught people and not student numbers.

"I thoroughly enjoyed the mandatory theology courses the university required of all freshmen. These courses were extremely stimulating and thought-provoking. It was during this period I learned things are not as simple as we may think or we might have been told. In essence, this was the beauty of Mercer. They taught students how to think rather than what to think.

"On campus, our daily lives were ripe with structure and chaos. It did not take long to grow up at Mercer. This was the students first, foremost, and free course. You learned self-sufficiency and self-reliance. Discipline was the only area in which we could momentarily relax and be goofy college kids. This much-needed phenomenon occurred at every event other than academics. There were plenty of extracurricular activities like fraternities, social clubs, academic clubs, sororities, competitive team sports, tennis, basketball, football, softball, dances, parties, picnics, weekend excursions, dating, card games, school-sponsored activities, and more. Mercer knew how to keep us busy, hungry, and glued to books. We took care of the rest.

"My brother David, my daughter Faye, and I have only fond memories of Mercer University. It is an excellent institution run by professionals who care.

"Jonathan, as for my three buddies or partners, I'll start with Barry 'Big' Prat. I met Barry on the campus of Mercer University in Macon, Georgia in 1970. I was an incoming freshman, and he was a sophomore. We lived across from each other in the oldest dorm on campus

"Back then, Barry was from Lakeland, Florida. He had a cousin who was a famous singer and ex-beauty queen. For many years, she was a well-known entertainer. She used to do orange juice commercials back in the seventies and eighties. Her name escapes me.

"Back in the day, Barry's family owned orange and other citrus groves in this area of Florida.

"Without doubt, he is one of the most unique people I have had the pleasure to know. He is brilliant. I'd hate to guess his IQ, but I'd bet it's off the charts for genius. He can literally do anything.

"He's an accomplished artist, musician, and thinker with a true spiritual nature. In fact, I'd consider him to be sort of a savant. He was performing major concerts as a classical pianist at the age of seven. He has a photographic memory with total recall.

"You can ask him anything, and he'll take off providing more information than you had expected or wanted.

"He's an avid reader and a natural athlete with blinding speed and raw athleticism. He has the body flexibility of an angular circus performer.

"Barry has the ability to teach himself how to play and master any musical instrument he wishes. He writes music, paints, sculpts, and draws, using varied mediums. He is as current as the next day's paper on world events.

"You'll never meet a more free-hearted individual with a heart as large as New York City. Big always seems to have a fresh and different perspective on most subjects.

"His constant smile is infectious. With dark features, long, straight, black hair, and dark eyes, he smiles like a mischievous child on the edge of trouble.

"He can create art from anything. Back in 1971, I remember he saw a cover of an Allman Brother's album in black and white, and he was instantly inspired by it. Later in the week, he could be seen on campus rummaging through trash receptacles, looking for a template. He wanted a piece of solid plastic about the size and thickness of the album's cover or a little larger.

"He found it, and within a few short days, after using a pin and punching thousands of tiny holes into the plastic, he had created an exact replica of the cover art. It was a handmade silkscreen.

With it, Barry proceeded to make silkscreen t-shirts for his friends. He's a talented individual.

"Another of his cousins is Andrew Prine, a well-known actor in Hollywood, known for his western and bad guy rolls.

"Google him and read about his connection with one of the most notorious murders in the history of Hollywood — second only to the Black Dahlia case, in my opinion.

"A young, affluent, aspiring, and beautiful actress was found nude and murdered in her apartment. Her nickname was 'Cookie.' Her homicide remains unsolved to this day.

"Reportedly, a young college co-ed may have played a mysterious cryptic role in the case with an appearance on a popular Chicago TV program. The host of this show was a famous celebrity in Chicago during this period. The college co-ed later became a First Lady of the U.S. Read the stories. Whether true or not, they're fascinating.

"It is a matter of public record Andrew Prine was an early suspect, seeing he'd gone with Cookie. Before her murder, he'd recently broken it off with her. Eventually, he was cleared by homicide investigators.

"As I said, Barry has a photographic memory. As a young boy, he appeared on the *I've Got a Secret* TV show in New York. None on the panel guessed his secret. He had total recall of every aspect of every baseball player represented on Topps Baseball cards. He could tell who the player was and all his statistics from just seeing a random body part of the player.

"He's the closest human to a walking and breathing Wikipedia I know.

"He can spin a tale from nothing... a yarn worthy of print and sell. His stories, life's experiences, and interpretations of life are interesting, informative, and often humorous.

"He is retired, unemployed, and sixty-two years of age. As he would say, he gambles for a living.

"Just today he said, 'Rod, it would not surprise me at all if soon they discovered at the southern axis of Earth a wooden stick protruding from the axis. The Earth is nothing but a huge lollipop. It has been licked by the universe since the beginning of time. The aliens from all points, inner Earth, and beyond can't get enough of it. They frequent our planet in search of her sugary sweetness. They lick away. Take a lick or two, Rod. Yep, our big blue planet is a huge sucker.'

"This is Barry Prat whose friends call him Big.

"Next, there is Matt 'the Ringer' Ringer. I also met Matt at Mercer University back in 1970. He is from the rolling hills of North Haledon, New Jersey. His dad was from New York and his mom from Georgia — hence the southern college connection. Matt was Barry Prat's roommate and pal for life in everything and nothing in general.

"They wrote articles for the Mercer University paper. If my memory serves me right, they won 'Best Room on Campus' two straight years. The first year, they won it because of their room decorations of neat band posters, t-shirts, personal art, and general overall coolness.

"The second, year they went back to basics. For at least a quarter, they stripped their room bare like it was vacant. But they lived there. Nothing was in view but empty desks, two bare mattresses, no pillows, and two chairs. For this unique approach and due to the hardship for their efforts, they won the prize back to back. The article and pictures in the Mercer Bears paper were stark, funny, and quirky like them.

"Matt is a tall man. He is semi-retired after having to sell a once lucrative family business due to New Jersey's oppressive business regulations, unions, cheaper foreign competition, and business taxes. After many decades, he had to sell their family business.

"Matt did not play any of the usual sports. Instead, he fancied a good game of pool while smoking and drinking longneck bottles of cold beer.

"In many ways, he was a an interesting introvert, but when he said his peace, it was always apropos, usually prophetic, and always as blunt as cold steel barbed with righteous indignation, humor, or both. He cut to the center of things.

"The Ringer was the embodiment of the 'keep on trucking' character from the 1970s. He would have been a natural at any *Grateful Dead* concert.

"He previously worked part time for fun at a local Jersey Shore bait and tackle shop. Along with his other duties, he ran a regular fishing report site on the Internet. As well as the shop, his residence was hit by the last New Jersey storm. Both were wiped out.

"He and his wife also owned a country log home with acreage in the mountains of New York. Reportedly, their land rests on a vast amount of natural gas ready for fracking. Yet again, the government knew best, stopping the research and development in its tracks.

"They have since relocated to metro Atlanta.

"Matt is also an artist with a dry wit and laid back nature. He is politically astute and knowledgeable in general subjects.

"He is an excellent writer and would make a superb political editorialist for any newspaper.

"Matt was a great match for a genius roommate. He would suggest their room held two. He is from excellent stock. Jon, in many ways, I'd say his mom and dad were like yours. His Harley-loving uncles could be a lot of fun, too. Matt subscribes to the *'live to ride, ride to die'* creed. He has always been a Harley man.

"Last but certainly not least, there is Jim 'Pops' Warner, who has been one of my closest and dearest friends. He is a good bit older at sixty-nine than me and a hell of a lot more crotchety.

"He is also retired from the Atlanta Police Department where he attained the rank of major. This rank is close to being chief of the department. In a humorous way, this fact frightens me.

"He is a bright man — too bright at times — with keen senses and insights.

"He is a father of two daughters. They are in the medical field, and they're graduates of Auburn University. Jim was raised in Florida around Bradenton. In youthful bliss, he enjoyed all the amenities of Florida life with water always in play. As a young boy, he loved the outdoor life, dogs, sport shooting, hunting, fishing, reading manly type books, and periodicals related to the subjects. To this day he enjoys the same things.

"He is a handsome man, or so I've been told, and like Robert Redford's character in the movie *The Way We Were* most things, including women, came too easy for him. But unlike Redford's character, Pops hasn't realized or acknowledged this fact... notwithstanding my constant reminders of such to him. Needless to say, as a young man in Florida and as an adult with the APD, he had no problem with finding the company of ladies. They would flock to him then as they do now at sixty-nine. Finally, he's showing a few faint signs of aging.

"For many years, he and I have fished and hunted together.

"Pops likes card games, enjoying Bridge and really any game requiring thought. He's pretty good at the stuff. Jeopardy is no match for him.

"Jim Pops Warner, has an unbridled love of nature and animals. I cannot count the times he has personally rescued a turtle in the roadway, a stray cat, or dog. His fishing needs some help, though.

"Pops is always up to an adventure or a mission as we used to say. He's game for anything in nature where he can poke a stick at me the whole time.

"He lives alone in Douglasville, Georgia with plans to move in the future to Widowee, Alabama or the Pensacola area of Florida. He resides close to his oldest daughter, son-in-law, and grandkids.

"His youngest daughter is married without children living in Birmingham, Alabama. Often, Pops and his pets visit both daughters. He is one of the best fathers I have ever known, and his girls adore him... as they should.

"He's a frugal but generous kind-hearted man who has helped me, Rose, and Faye on more than a few occasions in the past thirty years. Jim can be depended upon, and he has always been there for me. I can only hope he can say the same for me.

"Jim is a one-of-a-kind true friend. My only advice to the general public would be to beware because this old dog will hunt.

"I am the only person authorized to give him a little razzing or at least, willing and able to tell him the truth about himself.

"It's a wonder he has not knifed me. As some say on the force, Jim's a good egg!"

In Jon's presence, I made the phone calls to my three friends with the exact instructions he had advised. To my surprise, they were unusually receptive to all of my suggestions. They'd do as they were told — a second miracle in one day.

A Step Closer to Objective Consciousness

In preparation for the arrival of my partners, Jonathan and I had agreed to arrive early the next day. This day would change their lives forever. I advised him I suspected they would also be early. So, we set 8 AM as our arrival time.

The night before, sleep did not come easily. Problems ran through my head as I worried about my role in changing so many lives within my inner circle. At the same time, worry and dread about what our tasks would be stole my rest. My improved brain was multitasking wildly in all kinds of negative ways.

Rose and Faye were my greatest concerns. It was one miserable night. The only way I could rest my mind came when I started to concentrate on the blackness from my journey and the light that led me to Paradise. The soothing sounds of the gentle waves, cascading against the sugar like sands of Heaven's beach, did the trick. At last, I slept like the dead for a few hours.

I arrived at the garden about 7:45 AM. Jonathan was already there, sitting on our bench with pen and paper in hand. He was back to his writing, and this was a good sign.

"Good morning, Jon, do you mind if I call you Jon?" I stated.

"Good morning to you, Rod. Sure, call me Jon. I like Jon, and it's much easier on the tongue and ear like Rod, I suppose," he responded.

It was clear he had slept well the night before and had arrived in a creative mindset.

"Now, let's get to work. We have a lot to cover before they arrive. As we discussed, I will reveal myself after you have had some time to chat with Jim, Barry, and Matt. At first, try to keep the questions down since you and I can explain things to them once their questions begin. I will introduce myself to them.

"I've been sitting here for a while working on some of the logistics of our orders. Like I've said, each of your friends will be tasked with managing seven fellow ushers to assist in these jobs. We need to go to the tree now for further instructions and details of our parts in this," Jon advised.

Jon and I walked under the tree, but before we looked up, I was compelled to say, "Can we both take the journey simultaneously?"

"Sure we can. In fact, before it is over, there will be no limit as to how many can experience it at the same time. Now, clam up and look up. We have work to do," Jon ordered.

We did and shot like a rocket up to the top of the tree. Looking to the heavens, a huge puffy cloud in the color of a sailor's red sky warning appeared. From this motionless cloud, a pleasant male voice stated, "Three must become the twenty and four in two weeks from today.

"Your ushers will have two weeks to accomplish this first phase of their journeys. Each of the chosen three partners will be provided with a list composed of seven names to be penned by Jonathan with your input, Rod. You will know many of the chosen but not all.

"Jonathan has not been advised, but each of these twenty and four will be given the responsibility of ushering people to their trees for the journey.

"These new parcels will look exactly as this location. They will be placed on every continent — located near large urban areas of the greatest populations. Some continents will have three locations. Larger continents with greater populations will have more.

"The three will be strategically located and act as regional supervisors in charge of the other twenty and one under their charge.

"Rod, you will be the guardian over all and usher of this location. You are manager of the entire operation.

"When the time comes, you will ensure this location and the others around the world are ready for the masses. There are further instructions you will be given before we go viral internationally. The technology of the day now permits us to reach literally everyone in the world. All will be invited to come. Our goal is to reach every person on Earth, allowing them to experience this miracle. If we fall short in this huge endeavor, souls may be lost. Ultimately, many will not participate. It is their prerogative.

"From this point on, Jon and Rod, you must know time is not on your side. Things are changing and will be moving quickly. Within three weeks, each portal location will be up, manned, and operational. Many problems will arise. There will be more problems than you or your help can anticipate, but you will notice many of the people on the lists given to Jon are ex-police and ex-military. They are all retired. They are my gray usher brigade.

"This tree will be their initial portal of transportation to their cities. When they are sent to their worksite locations revealed to them initially only by GPS, their gardens will already be there. At any time, any of the trees will instantly transport one or all of you to any other tree within the network.

"Once the general public begins to come and after seeing what you have seen, thousands at each site will volunteer to help in any way possible. The public will not receive the physical attributes given to you. Tell your team to use as many volunteers as they need, but use them wisely with security and mission integrity in mind.

"Jon will tell you about the material support he has established in all the locations of the gardens. Your needs will be fulfilled. Do not worry about the clothes on your backs, shoes on your feet, or food. All things material and spiritual will be provided. Let your team members know I am always with them. Turn to me with their troubles... of course, this is after they've first turned to you two. You can and will solve all their problems.

"Organization, teamwork, shared goals, and selfless dedication are keys here.

"When it begins in three weeks, the crowds will quickly grow, exponentially. The masses to Mecca, Woodstock, the totality of yearly NASCAR races, and the Super Bowl pale in comparison to the numbers to come. Around the world, billions will come.

"Be prepared for anything. You will have armies literally and figuratively at your disposal.

"Rod, as Jon has informed, you are the only ones who'll speak directly to me. I am here for you. It is as simple as praying when you need me. I will answer you.

"Jon, you have been a faithful and true servant for all these years. You have performed all I have asked and more — admirably and without question. I must call on you once again. Rod and I need for you to stay longer.

"Know this, Jon and Rod, and convey my words to the twenty and four, your names will be exalted and praised for eternity. You and yours will have favored rooms in my house. You have been given the most critical and difficult tasks I have asked of any of my children.

"There is a well-known parable from one of my sons offered to his disciples a little over two thousand years ago. Loosely interpreted, it tells the story of a man who came to my son and asked if he would allow him to follow him. He was welcomed with the instructions to follow now, to leave his family, belongings, loved ones, and old life behind. The man hesitated with the revelation his father had recently died. First, he had to attend to his funeral. My son replied, 'Let the dead bury the dead. Let the living follow me.' In other words, let the unconscious bury the unconscious, and let the conscious follow the conscious as my son was surely conscious... on the path of objective consciousness. Let him with ears hear, and let him with eyes see. Not many see or hear.

"You and Jon have been on the path. Your job is to convince the twenty and four to come and follow. Your help will soon join you. In fact, the three are on the deer path now."

Then, within a snap of a finger, the cloud was like a drive-in movie screen, and we were shown what was to come. We saw the meeting with the three, the subsequent meeting with the other team members, and their transport through this portal to their sites all over the globe. We saw the masses coming and going in peace and tranquility. We saw the world at the threshold of transformation. It was a beautiful sight to behold.

Jon and I were sent back into our bodies. He went behind the huge trunk of the tree, and I sat on the bench, waiting for my friends to enter the garden.

It was a glorious day.

Three to the Tree

The guys were early.

They entered the field from the deer path in full laughter. It was a nervous laughter.

I walked over and greeted them with a handshake and huge bear hug. This was our usual greeting way.

Immediately, Barry was the most impressed and exclaimed, "WOW!"

As we all walked towards the bench, Jim looked around.

Matt was, well, Matt... never too excited or easily impressed and always cool as hot ice. "Not bad. Not bad," he said.

Barry was instantly drawn to the tree. Once we'd reached the bench, he left the group and started to walk towards it in a trance with his eyes fixated on the massive greenery with trunk and limbs. "Not yet, Barry. Not yet," I ordered, as I faked my normal or usual sixty-two-year-old-bad-knee hustle over to him, taking him by the arm and leading him to the bench.

At this juncture, Jim and Matt were discussing the business potential for the whole area. So far, they had it subdivided with the centerpiece of the property being the tree. A sizable lake was off to the right where the land begins to gently slope towards the eastern wood line. There would be custom built homes, dotting the pastoral landscape and starting in the low $700,000 to $1,000,000 range. The tree would become the central attraction of a circular park with a Victorian gazebo, sidewalks, benches, and garden for the residents. The housing crash would have no adverse effect here.

"Do we own all this open land and tree?" Jim asked.

"Well, yes and no, but technically, yes for me and no for you three right now," I answered.

"Eventually, each of you will be in possession of an exact twin of what you see before us," cryptically, I added. This was starting to be fun.

The fun ended.

Matt jumped in with, "Rod, I was under the impression each of us had twenty-five percent ownership of this purchase. How many acres are here, and does this include any more acreage, including and beyond the tree lines bordering all four sides?"

"As to the total acreage and ownership or not, these things do not matter, or better yet, all of this will be thoroughly explained to each of you in due time. Each of us will have one of these tracts or gardens," I said, fully extending my arms and trying to encircle the entire area.

Barry added, "Guys, none of this is for sale, not one blade of grass or leaf from this magnificent tree. We are not to harm this garden in any way. Can't you see it and feel it? It is so thick I can even smell and taste its sweetness. Jim, Matt, stop the dollar signs chatter, and realize we are on holy ground — if not holy, surely sacred. Open your eyes and see. Open your ears and hear. Open your hearts and feel it!"

"There he goes again, Matt. Barry's on a spiritual trip. He will be seeing ghosts and goblins next," Jim stated.

"No, Jim. I don't think so, not this time. I believe him. Your eyes are definitely open but sight escapes you. This is a special place indeed," Matt responded.

"Jim, they are absolutely right. All of what they have said is true and gospel in more ways than you currently realize. Remember, I promised you a story and a miracle and each will come," I added.

At this point, Jonathan walked from behind the tree and over to the bench. He introduced himself to the guys, and they shared introductory chat.

Immediately, beginning with his age, Jon advised, "I am four hundred and eighty years old. Rod and I have become close friends in less than forty-eight hours. Soon, you and I will also be close friends. I will share with you our stories of how we met and what has transpired since. We will tell you all you need to know at this time.

"In the near future, you will receive further instructions as to what is expected of each you. We know you have a plethora of questions, but at this time, please, hold them since most of your concerns will be answered on your journey... the miracle. But let it be known and fully understood, neither you nor your lives will ever be the same."

I had not seen Barry so excited since 1970 at Mercer University. Truly, I felt he had some knowledge of what was to come. He couldn't help himself. He had to blurt out, "This is it, isn't it, the Tree of Knowledge from The Garden, the Holy Grail, Ark of the Covenant, and everything else rolled into one? Rod, isn't it? Isn't it?"

With a twinkle in his eyes, Jon stated, "Rod, take Barry to the tree first. I'll sit here with the boys. They can watch and wait for their turns — Jim, ye of little faith but remember '*He who is last will be first, and he who is first will be last*' applies here."

I walked Barry over to beneath the tree's branches. I told him he must be touched by me to take the trip.

At this point, I advised, "Barry, now look up, and tell me what you see?"

"Just huge limbs, tons of leaves, and the body," he answered.

"Look at me," I ordered, and he did so. I touched the sleeve of his shirt and said, "Now, look up."

He did and off he went mind out of body like a bullet in zero gravity. I could see all the colors bouncing all around, up, down, right, left, and sideways throughout the tree. I walked backwards from the tree to the bench.

Before the touch of Barry's sleeve, Jon had handed Jim a stop watch and instructed him to start the watch as soon as Barry had looked up again. Jim had done so.

In disbelief, Jim and Matt were frozen on the bench. Their senses were bombarded by what they were witnessing.

At this moment, Barry reached the top and the beam shot up to the heavens in full NBC Peacock colors. Almost as soon as his light touched the heavens, the beam ascended just as fast into the top of the tree, and Barry was back. For a few moments, he stood there weak in the knees. Beneath the canopy, he sat down on the cool green grass.

I went over and helped Barry to his feet, walking him over to the bench. He was speechless.

Jon told Jim, "Read the watch."

Jim exclaimed, "One second ticked off. This is impossible!"

"Well, are you sure your name is not Thomas?" Jon replied.

Jon told Jim, "Keep the time again when Matt looks skyward."

Jim was certain the stop watch was broken. So, he tested it several times before the others made it to the tree, finding it to be working fine.

While walking to the tree, I could hear Jon giving instructions to Matt. They stared into each other's eyes, standing beneath the limbs. Jon gave Matt a hug, and Matt looked skyward. Rocket two shot to the heavens. The tree came alive in full Technicolor. Again, Jim watched in amazement as similar movements occurred, and the light at the top shot up. It drew back as quickly, and just like clockwork, Matt was back.

Jim stopped the watch, and one second had ticked off. At minimum, he was certain each time the trip seemed to last a half hour or so in real time. While I led Jim to the tree, he remained confused, doubting his eyes and the watch.

Slowly, we passed Jon and Matt, walking towards the bench. Matt was moving like the dead in total zombie face and body language. At any second, I fully expected him to chant, *"Brains, brains."* He also sat quietly on the bench beside Barry. I noticed tears running down their cheeks.

Walking to the canopy, Jim seemed frightened and hesitant. Nervously, he asked if I was going to touch him too and added, "This is no funny business thing, is it?" Briefly, we laughed. I said, "No, nothing like it." I gave him a big hug and said, 'Now, look up you old fart.' He did and off he zipped.

Matt, Barry, Jon, and I watched his journey from the bench, and zap, he returned to his body, falling to the ground in full fetal position. He was crying profusely and pleading for God's forgiveness. He regretted his doubts, begging for the rooster not to crow three times. We all heard these words.

Jon and I went over, helping Jim to his feet.

Jon tried to console him and said, "Jim, each trip is unique and personal. All of ours was as well, and what you experienced and saw was just for you. Grow from it."

We returned to the bench. The three were drained. Nobody spoke for ten or fifteen minutes. Smiles began to creep on the faces of Jim, Barry, and Matt. The tears were wiped away and euphoria was kicking it.

Jon said, "Endorphins."

I chuckled, "Endorphins, dude."

Jon broke the ice and advised, "Time is short. We have plenty of work to do and only fourteen days to complete it. No questions right now. They are to be answered by Him." Jon pointed at the tree. He led all of us back under the tree and said, "We are going to take a ride together. Please, form a circle, and touch the elbow of the person next to you. When I close the circle, look up."

We made the circle as Jon instructed. We later learned touching would no longer be required once we were on location. But for some reason, I liked doing it.

At this point, Jim responded, "Back to the mountain, Rod."

The five of us looked up.

Effectiveness Is the Measure of Truth

A man-sized tub of fluffy buttered popcorn and a super-sized drink of our liking were waiting for us as we sat down in our seats. We had entered the portal the usual way, but this time, the five of us landed in a small theater like those you see in the personal screening rooms of the large movie studios.

It was comfortable, sitting there in the semi-darkness, looking up at the screen before us. All of my friends and I share a deep-rooted historical love for popcorn. No sooner than I had taken a big swig of my soda to wash down a huge handful of buttery corn, a voice behind us, sounding strangely like one of a famous deceased actor said, "Roll it!"

The screen lit up with an advertisement for the concession stand like we used to see at the drive-in back in the 1960s and 1970s. It was complete with the marching band composed of the lollipop drum major, a large orange drink with a striped straw, and exploding popcorn used like confetti, popping all around the marchers. Barry almost choked on his corn when the music and delectable parade began. As some used to say, we "cracked up from the floor up. The laughter was deafening. For our new arrivals, the ice had surely been broken... for all of us.

This shameful display of absolutely hilarious commercialism was followed by a Salty Pete the Sailor Cartoon custom made for us.

Salty Pete was sent on a mission to save his anorexic sweetheart, Miss Ruby, who had been kidnapped again by her other suitor, Crabby Mike. Mike had taken her to a deserted island. It was awfully close in appearance to what I had seen in Paradise. Like there, the landscape, ocean, and beach were spot on.

Meanwhile, Salty Pete fought angry seas en route to save his love, Miss Ruby. She whined, "Oh, dear, oh, dear," screaming at the top of her lungs with mouth agape, "Help, Salty, help!" This was followed by another pair of "Oh, dears."

It didn't look like Salty was going to make it this time. His tugboat was smashed to pieces by giant waves and howling winds. Fate intervened. Salty was barely saved, using a floating wooden box which contained a few cans of his favorite energy drink. It was going to be close for Miss Ruby.

The storm subsided. Gentle waves washed Salty Pete onto the Paradise island beach. He was sprawled face down on the glittering sand. It was strange. The sand didn't fill his nostrils or gaping mouth. Salty was pooped and decked.

He could hear Miss Ruby, screaming in the distance, "Help, Salty, help!" In a wink, he sprang to his feet, grabbing a nearby can of energy drink, gulping it down. In a twinkle, he became a super caffeinated sailor with uber strengths. His flexed arms had bulging muscles in the shape of two volcanoes. His teeth were tightly clinched as his battle cry sounded like a factory's steam horn at quitting time.

He could see Miss Ruby at woods edge which bordered the beach. She was tied to a tree... strikingly, similar to our tree. Island natives had placed sticks of dry wood around her feet, and they carried lit torches.

Wickedly, Crabby Mike sat nearby, laughing from a raised throne made of bamboo.

In supersonic speed, Salty Pete made it across the beach and into the crowd of bloodthirsty natives.

Miss Ruby looked like a dressed praying mantis tied to the massive trunk of the Tree of Knowledge.

Salty Pete made short work of the natives. Each was knocked skyward across the island and into a distant active volcano — "Serves them right," I thought.

Then, it was Crabby Mike's turn. In this cartoon, the battle went on for a good spell... up and down the beach and all around the tree.

Miss Ruby tried to blow out the torches and stacks of burning wood. Pieces of the wood had caught fire due to the loss of a torch when Salty Pete blasted its holder into the angry volcano.

Time was of the essence. Miss Ruby was in dire peril. She would surely go up like a dry matchstick in the desert in June.

Salty Pete was losing the fight. Crabby Mike had his number this time. "Help, Salty, help!" Miss Ruby screamed. He glanced her way, and saw the fire growing too close to his love.

Crabby Mike continued to pummel him. Then, as divine intervention would have it, Salty Pete pulled a concentrated small bottle of Whoop-em energy drink from his front pocket, sucking it down. Well, you know what happened next.

Salty made short work of Crabby Mike, and when he threw his last big right, Crabby Mike was knocked into the sea. Both eyes were blackened and x'd out. Little drunken sparrows tweet tweeted all around his head.

A smiling blue whale surfaced and water shot from his blowhole, extinguishing the fire for Miss Ruby. Simultaneously, he swallowed Crabby Mike whole with a smile on the whale's face before diving back into the water.

Salty Pete rushed to Miss Ruby, cutting her loose from her bondage. They embraced as Salty Pete nervously said, "Aaaack, aaaack, aaaack," followed by a few guttural laughs through his firmly clinched teeth.

At this point, the couple looked into the tree and shot up through the branches... body and soul."

The End!

We clapped and laughed. Matt shouted, "Right on, Salty Pete."

Obviously, our Creator is exactly as billed — creative with a keen sense of humor and a large helping of self-deprecation.

We perceived the cartoon's meaning. Its hidden messages did not escape Jon or me. At this stage, we knew a little more than my friends. In this unprecedented adventure, there will be many perils, rough seas, temptations, and problems galore, but like Salty Pete, we will prevail. Everything is going to be okay.

At this point, we did not have a clue what to expect next, but whatever it was, it was going to be good. We were totally at ease and actually, having fun for a change. Jon and I knew the R&R was needed. This was a clever method of introduction and dissemination of pertinent information for our new recruits. I hope the twenty and one, as the voice called them, will adapt as easily as Jim, Barry, and Matt.

Next, an old stage and screen actor appeared bigger than life. His name escaped me at the moment, but I knew he had starred in many fine movies for lots of years. Possibly, our host is protecting us. He knows best. I learned later the actor's name was blocked from us for unknown reasons, and he would not be the last. He was tall, thin, and lanky with gray hair. He spoke slowly with a minor soothing drawl.

He welcomed us with, "Good morning, men. I'm sure you know who I am. I've been given the honor to host this tutorial for you. Before the lights are switched on here, you will learn all that is necessary to know at this time. Most of this will be redundant and otherwise repetitious for Jon and Rod, but I'm sure they won't object one bit. Plus, there is new information for both of them. So, pay attention. Here she goes."

Abruptly, he added, "The first presentation you will see is historical in context. This short piece will show each of you how and why you were chosen, providing a look back to date explaining how and why each of you made it to this point.

"You will see how all of this started and be given the minor particulars on a few of the guardians chosen before Jon and Rod. Jim, Matt, and Barry, you and the twenty one to come will be ushers. Jon and Rod, the guardians, are sort of equally in charge of the entire operation. They will also play an usher roll when 'day one' arrives. You three ushers will be regional supervisors in charge of your assigned seven ushers. Each of you, soon to be a total of twenty six, will be the keeper of a portal exactly like the one which brought you here.

"Jon, I can sense your unease at this time. We will talk later.

"Roll it, boys… Roll it, boys! Forgive me, guys, I've got three clowns on loan from the early days running the machinery back there and doing it rather poorly as you can see."

In an instant, the screen showed all the things promised to us by our movie star host. We also saw minor information about our families which was pleasant and unexpected.

Our unrecalled actor reappeared on screen and stated, "Jon, Rod, Big, Pops, and Ringer, I had to use them. I love nicknames. Why, back in my day, everyone in Hollywood had nicknames… had a few myself. Want to know what we called the short idol of the matinee who played gangsters? We called him 'Pecker' because the guy was one."

The recognizable voice of the fat clown came from the control room, "Get on with it, 'Stretch,' we've got things to do."

'Stretch,' our actor, stammering as he often did on screen and off, went back on target, "Next, this is especially for the new guys, but Jon and Rod, you also might pick a few things up. You'll see a demonstration on all the improvements each of you has received during your first climb. I like to call it a climb. After all, men, it is a tree and you did kind of climb it each time… well, anyway, you will see a tutorial on what has been added to you… the necessary stuff

you will need in this gig. I also like to call it a gig — like this gig
I was called in to do."

"It would appear Stretch likes to ramble and speak in run-on
sentences. Both are fine with me. I tend to write and talk like
that," I thought.

The screen came to life with a wild-eyed character who Barry
said was a famous writer. A couple of the other guys didn't know
who he was either, but apparently, something crazy was in the
mix. The writer was waiting on us in the desert somewhere in
the southwest USA, possibly, Arizona or New Mexico. To me,
he looked like either a blackjack dealer in Vegas or a balding
California tourist on a deep sea fishing trip off the Gulf Coast
of Florida.

He said, "With the aid of a few volunteers from the audience,
let's ride."

He showed us what the tracker beam did to us when it ran
across our bodies on our first climb. While watching, each of us
took turns on screen, or at least our doubles on screen, demon-
strating our upgrades. Enhanced eyesight and hearing, complete
and total head to toe wellness for life, ninety-nine percent brain
capacity with power greater than any computer in existence,
unlimited mental multitasking abilities, (finally, Jim can walk
and chew gum at the same time, what a klutz), and the ability to
access, upload, and download anything needed available from
any computer or the Internet was given. Like *Star Trek* and *Flash
Gordon,* we could travel from portal to portal at any time when
needed by simply using the provided GPS coordinates.

I thought, "If the numbers were a hassle for Matt, all he had
to do was think of the city, state, and or country wanted and say,
'Portal me up, tree.' Mentally, just for fun, I started the countdown procedure for rocketing Jim anywhere I wanted to portal
him — like to one of Jupiter's moons.

It was back to business time for me. In addition, we received
telepathic communications skills with party line greater than USA

NSA capabilities, the ability to travel in an instant from portal to portal when the other twenty four are in place, and a super libido, like on those pills but on call night or day around the clock. Apparently, Catholics were right all along on this one. He is serious about the whole procreation expectation.

I glanced down the line of seats and could tell the guys were also playing with their new mental toys. There were a few other upgrades but none as dramatic as those mentioned.

The writer dude then knelt in the desert, prayed briefly, and advised us, "In times of need, ask the cool Dude above or more appropriately, in those times when Jon or Rod couldn't fix it. He likes hearing from us all."

In his most serious sober voice, he also explained, "What follows is a binding legal disclaimer. So, Barry, Matt, and Jim, your complete attention is required. All present should know without doubt before the operation commences, 'Organized religion is not a requirement in any form or fashion for what is to come. Every man, woman, and child thirteen and over can see and hear the message. Children of a younger age will be protected at all times with age-appropriate messaging when necessary.'

"Our first goal of this phase is not to frighten. Atheist or Pope and all between will have access. We are all one in creation with our God — whomever God may or not be. A shepherd before us said, 'Let all who thirst drink.' In a short period of time, they will drink in the billions. One last vibe in closing, take heed, there will be no fear and no loathing here. You're the final shepherds of the flock."

With this ending, the desert and the writer exited screen right. Immediately, Stretch was back.

He said, "Now, the last thing you will see and it has been decided the twenty one to come will receive this same or a similar tour in fourteen days from today. Their Friday, we will see the simulation of the entire operation as it will unfold. There will be twenty six of you managing twenty six portals around the world. As you will see, their locations have been strategically selected with safety as a top concern in the most populated and easily reached cities throughout the world. Again, the larger continents with the greatest populations will have more portals.

"Don't worry about language or cultural barriers which might exist. You can upload any language in seconds and speak it fluently. Upload complete reports on the peoples and customs of your area.

"After this final tour, Jon and Rod will stay behind for further instructions and all pertinent printed material for each of you. Of course, this all could be handled easier with use of your new improvements, but for the next couple of weeks, please, try to be and act normal... thus, the printed material thing.

"By the way, there will be a family picnic hosted down there at Rod's garden on the Saturday following the arrival of the new recruits. It is fifteen days from today. As some have said, 'Time is wasting.'

"Your immediate family members will be the first of the public to witness what the world will soon see. It's time to bring your families into the fold, and let them know what you have been called to do.

"For the picnic, all will be provided. You will be able to access the west end of the tract by car. Park there on the grass, please. it's impervious to damage. You're to invite immediate family members only which means father, mother, grandparents on both sides, sons, daughters, significant others, if applicable, grandchildren, brothers, sisters and their children, and last but never least, your pets are welcome. Pets are always welcome in His house."

Next, we saw how we would acquire our portals, and their locations were revealed. Jon was to man his new portal near the Hudson River. The North American continent would have four portal locations.

At this point, I looked at Jon, sitting next to me with a strained smile on his face.

Barry, Jim, and Matt's locations were strategically placed between the continents with the greatest populations for obvious
supervisory reasons to assist each of their seven. The plan looked
brilliant. It was shown Jon and I would be tasked with the mass
communications throughout the world, beginning on "go day" Sunday, two weeks and two days from today, Friday.

It was too fast. I was flooded with uncertainty. I stared at Jon
and could see he was equally troubled. With all we had seen, we
still doubted. I was ashamed of myself.

It was made known Jon had prepared the way for us. Earlier,
he had purchased all the plots of open land needed for the portals
and grounds, opening bank accounts in major banks in each portal city all over the world. This was done in each usher's name with
a hefty balance in them for operational and living expenses.

He had also procured a residence nearest the portals in each
city for every traveling usher. There were ample financial resources
provided for us. Mine was placed in the largest bank in Atlanta.

Jon had taken care of everything. Who was to take care of Jon?
He was under the impression he would be with his family by
now. My heart was breaking for Jon. If he must remain, where
was Jon to stay?

Then, it was over.

Stretch appeared a last time, thanking us for our attention and
service. He said, "It is a pleasure to know you. It's an honor and
a privilege to at least be a small part of your journeys. I wish I could
go with you.

"Pops, Big, and Ringer keep the faith, and you're headed back
now."

With a snap of Stretch's skinny fingers, the three vanished from
the screening room.

"Jon and Rod, hang around for a message to be followed by a
special screening," Stretch advised and exited.

The voice, as Jon and I had come to know it, came from the
direction of the control room. Thoughts of passages from the Old

Testament, Moses, Aaron, forty years in the desert, and the traveling temple came to mind. Obviously, to this day, the curtain separating God from man exists as it did for forty years within the traveling temple.

It was an overwhelming feeling to know Jon and I are privileged above all mankind to be in His temple, in His presence, and listening to His voice. Listening was easy. Hearing was a different matter. I prayed Jon and I were also hearing Him.

He said, "Jon, my son, I am sorry for what I must ask of you. I apologize. I grow old and now weary of all which I inflict upon you and your fellow man. By now, it should have been easier — better. For all mankind, things were supposed to be improving, and in small measure, I admit they have been. But my children have grown more and more thick-necked.

"The natural course of events is children will eventually grow into adults. Who among us has no appreciation of the folly in a child? Well, adulthood is not in the future for mankind, and destiny will not be altered for you. It's a done deal, Jon and Rod. It is finished."

At this moment, I thought, "With whom does my God wrestle?"

He continued, "Jon, you are called again. My plans were faulty. I am... fallible. I must have taken my attention off the population growth there. Another portal location was needed. Your new portal and plot will rest where the old one had near the Hudson. It is necessary.

"This is not an order. It is a request. If you wish, you can stay here today, and Rod can handle the rest. I will honor your wishes with no malice if you choose to stay or go. I have been the one to go back on my promises to you. Think about it for a little and let me know. Either choice is fine. If there is anything you need to help you decide, let me know. It will be given."

At this request, I prayed for Jon to stay, and I knew how selfish and cold it was.

After this, the voice was gone.

Then, Lucy appeared on screen seated in a rocking chair beside the large fireplace of Jonathan's home near the Hudson. She held a small child. Lucy was stunningly beautiful. Jon had described her to me exactly as she appeared here. Her skin, hair, and facial features were radiant.

Since this was personal, I stood to exit from the theater.

Jon caught me by the wrist and said, "No, sit down. I'm too weak alone."

I sat.

Lucy said, "Hello, my love. This is our son, Patrick. He lives as I. We are here waiting for you but worry not. Don't be troubled. Your time to join us will soon arrive, and we will be here together for eternity. Find comfort in the Lord. Find solace in knowing time means naught here.

"Seeing you today is but a brief moment removed from our last embrace — our final kiss. For you, I know it has been many lifetimes. My beloved, you are still needed among the living. We will have eternity to share. There is one last task to perform.

"We are all so proud of you, my darling. Please, respect my wishes, and see this to its end. It will come soon... quickly, like the Old Testament taught us, *'Like a thief in the night.'*

"Verily, your way has been forged. It has been made known to me a house on the land of your youth has been acquired for you. It is vacant and ready for your return. My dearest, think of me and Patrick as you relocate to our beautiful Hudson.

"I say this for I know with full heart you would not go against my wishes. My Jonathan, we three will be together shortly... yes, shortly."

And with this, she was gone.

Both Jon and I were crying. All the tears moments were sort of becoming too regular. But dang it, who wouldn't have been crying after seeing and hearing Lucy? You? Well, not me.

Jon stated, "Where are the keys to my new house?"

After his question, we were zapped back to our bodies. We were carrying maps, graphs, lists, keys, passports, bank checking books, and other paperwork. Jon was also holding a set of keys attached to one of those automobile tag key chains. It read,

"Jonathan Huna
1420 Hudson Mist Way
New York, New York."

Evidently, things had changed a whole lot in the last four hundred and fifty years.

Hopefully, Jon can help with a few of my questions about his experiences in the tree.

Jon's Heaven

I said, "Jon, I have a few questions for you. These questions have grown more important to me as our appointments above have escalated. We have discovered the trip has varied somewhat from person to person within our team. It is obvious each subsequent trip is more refined or tailored. The first climb has many similarities for all of us, but the climbs you and I have made together have been task-oriented without much else.

"You never actually told me how your first climb went back in 1563. I'm interested to hear what happened to or for you. Before we met, were your subsequent climbs the same? Did you have one-on-one sessions with the voice or God in similar cloaked fashion? Have you seen God? Has He ever touched you like a handshake or hug? Did you see Lucy and Patrick on your initial climb? Were you able to speak with any of your loved ones or any of those you encountered? Did you land on the beach like I did? Do you think..."

At this point in my questioning, Jon interrupted, "Slow down, Rod. Better yet, just stop. I can't keep up with so many questions at once. He can, but I cannot. Did you take your BP medication today? I will tell you all you want to know but no more questions. I think you will find the answers you seek will be revealed in the next few minutes.

"It is always prudent to begin at the beginning. So, let us mentally travel together back to 1563 to the day in question on the banks of the Hudson River. I arrived early this morning to my favorite fishing hole on the river. The stretch of water there was wide, deep, and shapely. The exact spot where I liked to fish reminded me of a thin-wasted lady with wide curvaceous hips followed by two Rubensesque legs, forking to my left on the river.

"There was a natural pool of slow-moving lazy water flowing just where the thin waist section met the river's wide hips. The pool was about fifteen feet deep, and the water was perfect in color, clarity, and cleanliness. On sunny days, you could almost see the entire bottom from the banks. Its bottom was speckled with large rocks and a couple of big sunken trees. This was my honey hole.

"Rod, you like to fish, and you used to write traffic tickets. I'm sure you know what 'honey hole' means in both contexts. Well, the fish also used to love the hole, but fish can be finicky on a good day. They were either lock-jawed or eating elsewhere.

"Rod, in general, you'd think most things will change dramatically over the centuries. To an extent, they do, but in more ways, they stay the same. Technology drives this false belief. I'll use something germane to our discussion as an example. I assume you have fished for catfish in the past. This is an easy assumption because every fisherman has at one time or another in his life fished for them. Many people still do with regularity.

"There is nothing more tranquil than lounging on a riverbank with cane poles lined up at your fingertips with the presentation of a hook and bait, waiting for a hungry fish to take a chance. As you know, they win a whole lot of times. I also assume you have used a cane pole to fish. Think of the bait you used for catching catfish. Have you used dough ball, bits of cheese and scraps of pork, mealy worms, red wiggler worms, or wasp larvae? I have fished with all of those things back in the sixteenth century. How did you skin your catfish? Did you nail their heads to a tree and skin away? See, things tend to stay the same.

"No matter what I dangled at them, they were not biting. I didn't mind, too much. We could find something else for dinner. About an hour before I met my tree man, the catfish supper bell rang. I could not catch them fast enough. They came two at a time — then, three at time on my line with three hooks. It was fast and furious. Like I have said, they were running small. As fast as they had started biting, instantly, they stopped when I landed fish number nineteen. I do not remember praying for a bite or two, but somebody knew precisely how many fish were needed. Dinner was saved with tree money to boot. I suppose money actually does grow on trees or in rivers. Rod, no doubt about it whatsoever, this was a miracle.

"After I signed the paperwork and we looked up, my entire body felt like it'd been shot from a cannon. My brain was doing the traveling, but at the moment, I did not realize this fact. I felt my whole body take off, but there was no external signs of resistance or force to such speed. I landed on the first limb, and I felt like a hummingbird in a full panic. I was looking in all directions at once. My body felt like it had tiny wings, flapping at impossible speeds. But I didn't feel stressed or overworked. The tree was my nectar. This stop lasted a short time, and then, I was off to other branches. Each one tendered something new.

"On my first climb, I did not receive the whole package of upgrades like you. My new toys were limited and restricted to a great degree to the technology of the day. You can imagine what I received. The abilities to write, think, reason, invent, and speak all languages were given. Literally, I could operate any new device I came upon. This helped a great deal in the printing and publishing aspects of my extended career. For example, I was able to write textbooks and language translations. Many of my dusty works remain in libraries and homes all over the world.

"My brain might have been at ninety-nine percent capacity, but a good eighty percent of it was wasted. If I had used it during my early years in the northeast, they would have burned me at the stake for being a warlock or being possessed by the devil.

"This new nation received many of my finest works or pieces of them. I usually do not brag, but the next time you read our Declaration of Independence or the U.S. Constitution, think of me. In parts, plenty of thinkers and writers then and before are represented in those documents. Back then, in print, ideas and thoughts were shared. The domain was so limited, helping explain the whole borrowing situation. Plagiarism wasn't a big deal.

"Political literature was the most simple to compose. It was the romance genre of the day. All a writer had to do was present facts and truths. Your works either dazzled voters or incited the rest in the country. Through print, your audience was greatly increased in political matters. In my humble opinion, the French Revolution occurred when a large enough majority of the people was finally made aware of truths and facts. They can be different.

"As I ponged higher and higher up the tree, I received what we all do on the first trip. I saw my life from the second of conception to the moment. Rod, when I was first conceived, I witnessed the initial explosion as the fertilized egg burst into life. It appeared to me as vividly as those Internet simulations of the Big Bang theory of creation. It was just like it. I watched the history of creation to the day. Creation also started as a burst of ever-expanding light from blackness... like I had in mom's womb. It was beyond incredible, and it's always with me.

"At least for me, this reveal has never interfered with what Darwin found. I was also alive for this. The simple logic which placates any doubts comes from the scoring practice within the game of golf. They don't ask you how you got there. They ask you how many. Rod, we know the score.

"I flew through the universe, and at the time, you have to appreciate what little we actually knew about the universe. I took copious mental notes while wonder after wonder slowly sped past. I also did some nonfiction and seemingly, fiction writing in this area.

"God is the ultimate muse.

"I entered the dreaded black space or more accurately, the total lack of space. I don't know about you, but for me it was totally like being in complete blackness which we've all experienced — those dark times when you can put your hand just beyond touching your nose and you still see nothing. Too much of this will really freak you out as you begin to get dizzy, disoriented, and scared to make the slightest movement. I was so happy to see the tiny beam of light in the distance. Did you notice while you thought it was so far away, you also felt like it was at the tip of your nose? Initially, I was cross-eyed, staring at the dot.

"As abruptly as my brief stay wrapped in the white light had ended, my Heaven arrived. Rod, figuratively, this perfect white light is how God feels to me. I could stay wrapped for eternity in that embrace.

"Heaven was an aerial view of the Hudson and the surrounding countryside. I knew it well. I flew like the geese along the flow of the river. At times, I just skimmed the surface, and at others, my altitude grew as the landscape expanded in all directions. I flew over all the settlers' farms. There was activity below, but I could not identify any of the forms. But there was movement below.

"In the distance, I could see lush floating oases, tall mountains, and waterfalls of various magnitudes. Many of the same plots of land and trees like ours here were present throughout the countryside.

"I arrived at our farm as a big orange sun dipped closer to the horizon. There was plenty of light left to see Lucy, carrying a pail of milk from the barn. At first, she did not see me. When she did, she dropped the full pail, but not one drop spilled.

"I ran, more accurately, floated towards her. During this, it appeared I was hovering just above the ground. I felt like a ghost. I drew closer to Lucy, and as I started to speak, I was dispatched back beneath the tree... no worse for the wear. My tears flowed.

"Over the decades, I have not climbed the tree like this. Early on, I refused to do it because I knew I would try and stay if I went home again. All of my orders were given by the voice. It was many years later before I fully realized the voice might be God's. I simply thought it was the tree, telling me what to do and how to accomplish it at every turn.

"Before we met, I did not travel here by the tree. This is funny, Rod. I was told by the tree, 'Be on time on the date given and get there by your usual fashion, using some of those frequent flyer miles.' When I reported to our bench, my tree and surrounding landscape were here.

"Years ago, I had purchased a large parcel of land here. I have an inside bit of local history for you. Developers were able to find me, and a decade or more ago, they wanted to purchase this land. They did not understand no. After four or five offers, they finally divulged their development plans. They wanted to build the Mall of Georgia here. I could have made a bundle. Their last offer was four million an acre.

"I, rather you, have two hundred acres here. I talked to the tree about it before it arrived at this location, naturally. But the voice had a good attitude about the whole affair. He thought it was funny. They relocated their mall. I purchased a condo in Buckhead, Atlanta to be near to this area for when our time came.

"The tree would nudge me in the directions it wanted me to go. It got kind of fun. Sometimes, we played a guessing game. The voice would appear and say, *'Guess what, Jon?'* Then, I would usually guess I was moving. More times than not, this was the answer.

"I've never 'seen' the Man. At times, I've seen shadows when the voice would pop up like in the *Pop Up Video* television show.

"He has never touched me, and I have not seen him much less touched him. Do you recall what happened when the Ark of the Covenant was placed on an oxcart to be delivered to the Is-raelites after Jerusalem was retaken by the Philistines? If not, en route with the 'holy of all holies' the road was filled with ditches. At one point, the Ark shifted, and it came close to falling from the cart. One of the men following the cart reacted and laid hands on it, trying to keep it on the cart. The guy vanished into thin air. Hence, the long poles provided per order to carry the Ark once it held the prized religious artifacts of the Israelites.

"Maybe, we are not supposed to touch God. But I would almost bet he has visited me as I slept from time to time. His presence during these times would seem real. I've 'seen' him in my dreams many times. Each time, he is different in appearance, but he is always old, wise, and distinguished-looking. He easily could be a character in any number of old movies.

"I had never seen Patrick in Heaven until you and I saw Lucy and him together. Eventually, after my first climb, I did conclude she must have had to milk the cow late in the evening for milk for Patrick. Maybe, she could not breast feed, or it was some other reason.

"When we first climbed together, I was given all the rest of my additional upgrades like you. The green-blue beam passed up and down my body for a second time, and we arrived together at our destination. I'm faster than you, Rod.

"Enough is plenty. I'm done. No more questions."

We greeted the three, laying on the green grass, staring at a robin egg blue sky and beyond.

Glorious déjà vu.

The World Is What You Think It Is

We hated to break up the guys as they rested in the thick grass and chatted silently with each other. I could only imagine what Pops and Matt were downloading from the net. At intervals, like *Beavis and Butthead,* all of the guys laughed at what their minds were seeing.

In full voice, Jon said, "Snap to, guys. We've got work to do." Smothered in urgency, life returned to our new normal.

I advised, "Gang, while having fun with your new toys, please, act as normally as possible around everyone else. Barry, I know that will be doubly difficult for you but try anyway. Pops, stop downloading those magazines. Told you Jon, Pops dog will hunt. I hope no women are on his list of seven because, if there are, we better reassign them at once."

We took the printed matter received earlier and handed each of the three a large packet. Each packet contained all the pertinent information they needed to complete their recruitment, such as names, addresses, phone numbers of their recruits, housing locations and instructions, bank accounts with checking, savings, and access debit cards, their passports, the locations of their portals, all their fellow ushers material packets, the timetable schedules, and other miscellaneous instructions.

This was the first time any of us had seen most of the mechanical aspects of the job before us. It is funny how papers in hand can make things so real. The reality and urgency were apparent.

Pops commented, "Why do we need all of this paperwork? Can't we take care of most of this using our Google goggles?"

Taking this one, Jon said, "You're absolutely correct, Jim, but for the time being, during this crucial phase, this is the way it has been ordered. You know, we take orders, too. Plus, all of this paper does add a stamp of certainty to our duties. I'd agreed earlier we wanted it this way.

"Many of those you will see on your lists have experience in policing, military, formal volunteer work, supervision, or small business ownership. You will also learn most of them have displayed many of the same traits you four have exhibited.

"Collectively, they have proven themselves under fire to be dedicated, caring, and selfless in many ways. All are team players who will take orders and follow them — almost all of them. One or two will give us minor problems. But more importantly, they will carry them out.

"You'll discover our rookies are quite a diverse group. So, get used to it, men. From this point on, we are on a mission. We have our orders, and each of us must supervise others throughout this ordeal. What we will accomplish here will be seen in the future as the most massive undertaking by so few in the history of man."

I said, "Guys, let's open our packets and discuss what we have to. Prepare yourself because in sixteen days from today we will be on our posts across the globe. It's coming soon.

"But hold on. Give me a brief moment to explain something.

"Pertaining to the family picnic on Saturday, just over two weeks from today, Jon and I are in charge of this event. So, this means you three are as well. Please, inform your recruits the family picnic will happen the day after you bring them here for their rookie-to-veteran-in-a-day training period. Let them know who they can and can't invite and about the other logistics of the day.

"We have decided to make it like a Sunday church gathering picnic thing. Tell everyone who has climbed our tree they, each family, must bring two covered dishes of food... preferably, a meat and a vegetable or salad dish. Takeout is fine as long as it's the KFC, Church's, or Popeye's chicken.

"Jon and I will make sure enough trash receptacles, tables, and chairs are here and provide the liquid refreshments... limited to iced tea, fresh lemonade, and bottled water.

"Pops, you tell number six on your list to bring the chips since, he has no family, and he has always, like most male single people, brought the chips to a family get together. Also, tell him two bags won't cut it. Buy a bunch. He's cheaper than you, Pops.

"Let them know this place is sacred. So, keep it clean. When it is over, we all will pitch in and clean the place like it was new way back when.

"Also, Jon will be welcomed and introduced as part of my family — my wild young nephew from the Hudson River, Rip Van Winkle the 5th. I'm just kidding. He'll still be Jon."

At this, Jim raised his hand like at police school and said, "May I ask a question, sir?"

"Uh, oh, I see this one coming. Go ahead, Jim," I answered.

"Are you kidding me? Are you serious? I don't have to look at number six on my list to guess who it is. *'Say it ain't so, Joe, say it ain't so,'* please, not him, Thomas James? Is Tom on my list?" Pops whined.

"Yep, the one and only is all yours, and you're going to have to deal with him. Pops, this isn't your dance to run. Like the rest of us, you will have to take orders and follow them to the letter. Doing it or going it your way cannot and will not be tolerated this time.

"This propensity of yours has already gotten me chewed out by the boss, seeing how, I recommended you. I have been chewed out before, but never by anyone like this man... THE Man.

115

"Frankly, you are a subordinate exactly like Jon and me. We do not need you or any of the others telling us every step of the way how to properly build a campfire. You have brought this on yourself, and if you cannot follow what we order, then, walk now.

"Thomas is your responsibility, and all of you are mine and Jon's. If you decide to table your ego a little, you will soon see what this is all about. Believe this, it will be well worth the effort," I said.

"Rod, please, can I swap with Matt or Barry, or can you scratch him outright, since I've got a friend or two in mind for the job? You know what he is going to do. Rod, you do realize it.

"He will ask a gazillion questions, want to change everything, and criticize every step we take.

"He never listens, doesn't play or get along well with others, and consistently, colors outside the lines. Thomas is as hard-headed as a south Alabama mule. You know if he were dying of thirst you couldn't lead him to an oasis of Miller Lite. His head is already in the top of the clouds.

"He's not comfy in his skin, but he does float a little inside it. He knows absolutely everything, and he will often remind us of this. He'd Google and Snoops his own dog's name rather than believe it — if it came from me. As a matter of fact, I fully expect him to Snoops verify the reality of this tree when he first sees it and an additional time, after he climbs it. He'll tell us they deem the tree and trip to be 'False.'

"Over the years, I have tried to help him dozens of times. If there was a brick headed towards his head and I said 'duck,' he'd answer 'merganser' as the brick knocked him cuckoo.

"He simply never listens. He thinks he's creative, and at times, he is or has shown himself to be, but you remember what happened with him in the past. Waxing creative on a work report is like tossing ethanol-free gas on a fire.

"Rod, he has the potential of being our doubting Thomas and Judas rolled into one... and his name is Thomas. Danged, you'll see. I'm just saying," Jim lamented.

"Jim, it was a brilliant bio on Thomas, but you missed a few key things. Thomas is extremely creative, intelligent, and most of all, caring. He is the kind of man who does many good deeds for his fellow man and animals without fanfare or bravado.

"He is a sensitive man with a heart which would rival anyone among us, and you will never see this. He speaks highly of you, Jim.

"Jim, do I need to invoke Sylvester at this time? Do you need to take your silly junk down the hall?

"If anybody can, you can handle him, and you can't transfer him this time around. It is called tough love, man, tough love... ye of little faith. I have it on the highest authority when all is said and done he among the twenty one will shine the brightest. So, enough already. Deal with it," I ordered.

I added, "Back to the picnic for one last thing, each of us will have a time before the day is done to take our families together to the tree. Children of all ages are invited to experience it with their family. If they are under thirteen, they will be protected with the utmost care. Jesus proclaimed not one hair was to be harmed or disturbed on the children. Don't worry about this.

"Please, gently prepare your wives, husbands, children, and other adults in your family before they are told to look up. This one is also important. During the picnic, before the tree visitation, let it be known nobody and we mean nobody can play on or in the tree. In fact, for any reason you can think of, make them stay away from it. Tell their parents it is strictly forbidden for insurance purposes or something. Keep them out of the tree. We may decide to rope it off or something before they arrive.

"Now, pertaining to your packets, I'll turn it over to Jon."

Jon advised, "Most of these papers and documents are self explanatory. The important things are your individual lists of seven and your portal locations. All of you have received accommodations centrally located for your group.

"Note, you will have some of the most populated cities in the world as your home base. We've tried to keep your individual

117

team of eight as close as possible, but within your group, a few may be on a different continent than you. Sorry, guys, this is the way it has to be.

"Rod will be located here within metro Atlanta where the busiest airport in the world is located. I will be near the Hudson in close proximity to New York City.

"At all times, we will be available for you, and likewise, you are expected to be there for us. Please, have your seven ushers come to you for anything they need addressed. You will be able to handle the large majority of these. We know this. So, sort it out. But what you can't accomplish or answer don't hesitate to contact either Rod or me. We will continue to have access to the boss. Now, study your lists."

>*Jim Warner — Mexico City, Mexico*
>Jane Cumberworth — Sao Paulo, Brazil
>Bill Baxley — Lima, Peru
>Robert Woods — Rio de Janeiro, Brazil
>Ben Holmes — Santiago, Chile
>Sue Swanson — London, England
>Thomas James — San Francisco, USA
>Jimmy Wilson — Madrid, Spain
>*Barry Prat — Tokyo, Japan*
>Arthur Lowe — Shanghai, China
>Janet Bishop — Istanbul, Turkey
>Brian Crowley — Mumbai, India
>David Ashley — Beijing, China
>Candice Long — Deli, India
>Herbert Dill — Seoul, South Korea
>Jack Dupree — Tianjin, China
>*Matt Ringer — Moscow, Russia*
>Carol Burns — Saint Petersburg, Russia
>Tom Mix — Berlin, Germany
>Ashley Carter — Johannesburg, South Africa

Rudy Moore — Kinshasa, D.R.O.T. Congo
William Kane — Largos, Nigeria
Zach Milton — Cairo, Egypt
Ford Eds — Sydney, Australia

Jon continued, "As you see, we have everything to get moving. The clock is ticking. Please, table any questions to a later date. We have our orders. You can contact Rod or me at any time. You have fourteen days from today to report back here at 9:00 AM with all your recruits. Initially, be guarded what you tell them, of course, but tell them the truth.

"Remember, eventually, the worldwide masses will come in the millions to each portal. We came, and they will, too.

"As to your team members, the promise of a living miracle combined with a vital mission is too enticing. These you can promise them. Rod and I will see you hear at 9:00 AM two Fridays from now and don't forget the picnic instructions."

With paperwork in hand, the three departed. Jon and I walked over towards the tree. Picking a perfect spot, we laid on the cool October grass. I wouldn't swear to it, but I think he was snoring before me.

There Are No Limits

Jesus says... the Kingdom of God is inside of you, and it is outside of you. When you come to know yourselves, then you will become known, and you will realize that it is you who are the sons of the living Father. But if you will not know yourselves, you dwell in poverty, and it is you who are that poverty.

—Gospel of Thomas saying 3

I am the light that shines over all things. I am everything. From me all came forth, and to me all return. Split a piece of wood, and I am there. Lift a stone, and you will find me there.

—Gospel of Thomas saying 77

The last fourteen days flew by, and as I drove to the field from home, bizarre worrisome thoughts ran rampant through my mind. This was the Friday... the day of the apparent end of the beginning and a day before the picnic. Luckily, it is a short drive from my house to the tree. I entered the field, glancing at my tree, worrying. I parked. The clouds of doubt and anguish evaporated. This place has this awesome power.

It was 8 AM, and Jon was not here. Except for the first day, each day we've met for the past fifteen days, he has been waiting on the bench before I arrived. This was odd.

As I walked towards the bench, I heard a blast on a siren to my rear. Jon was pulling onto the grass. With blue lights flashing, a motorcycle officer followed him onto the field. As Jon parked his car, there was one more hit of the siren. Jon exited his car, waiting calmly, quietly for the Gwinnett County motorman's instructions. The officer dismounted his bike and placed his helmet on his seat. While walking towards Jon, he requested to see the usual items.

Slowly, I walked up. Jon produced his driver's license and proof of Insurance card.

"So, this is where you were headed so fast," said the officer. I did not recognize him.

I had lived in Gwinnett County for about 25 years, and I'd come to know a few county officers from the area — also from my APD days. On rare S.W.A.T. occasions, we'd cross-train with a group of their team members. Sometimes, I'd meet other G.C.P.D. officers at the State of Georgia Law Enforcement Training Center near Macon, GA. I had also supervised more than a few ex-Atlanta officers who had made the switch to the county. They'd recruited more a number of our good folks during a period in the 1980s. They'd raised their pay and benefits package above what was offered with Atlanta.

I did not know this officer.

As the officer began writing Jon a ticket, I walked up to them, introducing myself with a handshake to a nervous and suspicious officer. I knew the look and had used it on duty in such circumstances many times before. The officer continued writing.

"Sir, how fast was my friend going?" I inquired.

"Clocked him at fifty in a thirty zone," writing like mad, he said.

Then, it came, and I stated, "I live in the area, and I'm a retired Atlanta police officer. In fact, some of my guys are now with your department. Are Gibby, Harper, and Welton still on S.W.A.T.?"

Prior to this question, I had noticed his S.W.A.T. patch on his leather motorcycle jacket. Gwinnett S.W.A.T. operates differently than Atlanta's, or at least, they did back when I was on ours.

121

We had a full-time team with two shifts dedicated to tasks called upon for S.W.A.T. Atlanta needed a full-time S.W.A.T. unit with the crime statistics we had.

Gwinnett S.W.A.T. members had other various assignments on the force, and when necessary, they were utilized.

At this point, he stopped writing and with a guarded grin, said, "Sure, they are and me too for the past two years. Harper is now our commander, running the team."

"Yep, all those guys are good people. Seriously, tell them hello from Captain Travis. They might remember me," I responded.

At this, Officer Jacobs handed Jon back his license and said, "Sir, you need to slow down. I'll issue you a warning this time, but realize when you speed you jeopardize not only your life but other citizens and officers alike. We have to speed to chase you down."

Jon answered, "Thank you, officer. I will heed your advice and keep my mind on driving safely rather than the day's work ahead."

I smiled at Jon and said, "Do you want to invite the officer, a few of his fellow officers, and their families to the picnic? What do you think about it?"

"Sounds great to me, the more the merrier," smiling, Jon said.

"Officer Jacobs, we are having a group picnic here tomorrow with our families as well as many others who will be arriving by 0900 hours. There will be twenty six of us here today, and I would bet a Krispy-Kreme doughnut against a Ben Franklin you'll know many of them or at minimum, a few of them.

"Tomorrow, all of our families will be here celebrating. Please come by with your family, and also, invite your S.W.A.T. members with their families to come. You will have the time and experience of your life. We throw a good and clean party.

"It is a covered dish type thing. We'll provide the drinks, chips, and fun. Each family is bringing two dishes, but on such short notice, you guys can forego bringing food. There will be plenty. Seriously, do attend, and I'd love to see those guys again. Invite whomever you like. Police officers, their families, and their pets will always be welcome here," I stated.

"Thank you, Captain Travis. I might just do it. It was a pleasure meeting you. Have a good day," he responded, mounting his bike and snapping his helmet on.

"No, no, young man, the pleasure was all mine. We'll see you tomorrow — around noon will be the kickoff time," I answered in sincerity.

I joined Jon on the bench. He was shaking his head left to right and grinning like a jackass.

"Yes, there is a handshake, and it begins with mutual respect," I advised.

Almost silently, he sat, looking up at the tree.

"At any rate, thanks," he said in a little whisper.

Deep in thought, I sat there. Desperately, we'd needed the two week break before our new recruits arrived. During this lull period, we grew even closer. There was not much rest involved. It was a working fourteen days for us. There were things to do, loose ends to tie, preparations made for our next phase of training, and the picnic with miracles all around.

We had estimated the crowd could be as low as one hundred and fifty or as high as three hundred. Jon decided we should think three hundred plus, and I agreed.

He was able to procure use of all the tables and chairs we needed from Buckhead High Rise in Atlanta where he has a condo.

I purchased several new washtubs to be used for the tea and lemonade. We had all the details handled for the preparation work involved.

With so many suffering and out of work, it was an easy task to locate someone to grade a road. My brother-in-law, who I'd see later at the picnic, and his helper were hired to build a new gravel access road from the dead end of the dirt road to the edge of the field. The deer trail the three initially followed into the plot was perfect for the new road. We could park our vehicles on the grass at the western corner of the field.

We also decided to use one of those plastic temporary fences to encircle the tree outside the canopy. The fence could be easily removed before our families took the trip.

I said to Jon, "We're going to need those guys. I hope a bunch of them come tomorrow. This is the first garden, and their cooperation and security efforts could prove invaluable."

"I know. This is precisely why I made sure I was speeding when I passed the motorman on the side of the road with a radar gun pointed at me. I figured you'd invite them. After all, look at how many retired police folks will be on the turf in a few minutes," Jon responded.

By 9:00 AM, all expected had arrived. Suddenly, it looked weird to see this number of cars on the property. This bothered me... more than I had thought it would.

As we began the day, I requested each team of eight to sit together on the grass. I knew more than a few of those present. Some were subordinates of mine through the years, and a few were my supervisors at one time or another. A couple of them were friends from long ago in the neighborhood.

I was shocked to find one of the ladies was a close friend — a cheerleader who graduated from Roosevelt High School with me in 1970. Janet's name had escaped my attention. Naturally, she'd used her married name.

I later discovered her husband had died several years earlier from prostate cancer.

I explained to the team, "For those who do not know me, I am Rod Travis, and to my right, this is Jonathan Huna. We understand that Jim, Matt, and Barry had a rather easy time in recruiting you. In fact, all of you were aboard within three days.

"Actually, Thomas, you were the first to join us.

"We also have been advised the other eleven days were not wasted. Each team supervisor met with his group every day up to this meeting. To this point, I'm certain you've been given all of the details known by your leaders.

"In our past professional lives, each of us is familiar with the hierarchy within a company and rank system. A few of you also have business ownership experience. From this point on, look at us in this framework. Jon and I are in overall command of this operation. We are the majors. Your team captains are Jim, Matt, and Barry. You've been elevated to the rank of lieutenant for the main reason you are integral parts of management. You will also hear the terms 'guardian' and 'usher' used. This has been explained to you by your immediate supervisors, Jim, Matt, and Barry.

"All information will flow down from your supervisors to you and up from you to your immediate captains. In short, seek council with Jim, Matt, and Barry first and foremost. They will contact me or Jon, if absolutely necessary. Jon and I are the ones who have personal access to the boss. All of this will become clear to you soon. The first answer you seek is, 'Yes.' You'll receive everything you've been promised — more than you could ever imagine. Have faith and be patient.

"Folks, like I said earlier, this is Jonathan to my right, and he will take it from here, Jon."

"As Rod said, I'm Jonathan Huna. Call me Jon. I regret to advise I do not know any of you. This would be most improbable. Look at me like the great, great, great, great grandfather you never knew. I know I look much younger, but in fact, I am exactly four hundred and eighty years old," Jon revealed.

With this revelation, the crowd was visibly and audibly upset. Thomas rose to his feet.

"Calm down, gang, calm down. Sit back down, Thomas, now! Most of you know me, and I hope you know you can totally trust me. Jonathan Huna, the man before us, is four hundred and eighty years old.

"Shortly, you will learn his history as well as each of our individual histories... not by my voice or Jon's but through the tree behind me. This tree is as central to all of this as its location in this field. I know some crazy or minimally, strange promises have already been made to you.

"But consider faith and a dream brought all of you here like it did me sixteen short days ago. Can anyone say they did not have the most bizarre dream of their life the night before you met Jim, Barry, or Matt? Well, can you? I see no hand raised. So, I assume it was the same experience for all of us.

"Take a moment and visualize what happened in the dream. Is this the tree? I had it too the night before I met Jon on this field, staring up at the same tree which mesmerizes you here. This tree and some of its powers were shown in all of our dreams.

"In the interim, I have also learned of Jon's dream. Four hundred and fifty years ago, at thirty years of age, he left his home near the Hudson River. Quiet, please. All will be revealed," I said, in an effort to calm the new members.

Jon continued, "Well, let's see where was I... oh, have you received the information about the picnic tomorrow? Your presence and assistance are mandatory. We hope each of you'll take the offer to bring your immediate families seriously. It is guaranteed to blow them away — great miracles. For those of you who have not decided to do so, as directed, you must attend, but within the next ten minutes, you will change your minds. This, I guarantee. Girls and boys, it is tree time."

I said, "Everyone, let's go over to beneath the tree and gather in a circle. Please, hold hands in an unbroken chain, looking only at each other or if you wish, staring at the ground, but don't look up. When we get there and the link is formed, at this time and at no time sooner, we will look up into the canopy together when Jon says to do so.

"Trust me. You are not prepared for what is to come.

"No questions. Thomas, just for once, do as Jon says when he says it. You are going to love this experience."

As we made the connected circle under the tree, Jon said, "Look up."

Zap! Jon and I were transported to Paradise, sitting atop one of the glorious waterfalls, overlooking the soft rolling hills and valleys. To our immediate right the hills and valleys ran to the dunes, beach, and ocean.

Unimaginable pastoral splendor spread in all other directions. From our vantage point, we could see distant mountain ranges, numerous waterfalls of varying sizes, rivers, massive lakes, streams, and lush gardens.

Flowers blooming and trees laden with sundry fruits were prevalent. As I had initially seen, Oases floated slowly, effortlessly, near and distant throughout the landscape.

The colors were strangely different... intense, deep, and electrifying like pleasant neon lights.

Trees and their grassy plots similar to ours dotted the landscape in all directions away from the beach.

In the thick mist of the waterfall, Jon and I were shown the future events and how they would unfold.

My tree would be used first the next day by all of our families as well as around one hundred others from the county police department.

Sunday, the following day by 10 AM sharp, Jon, Jim, Matt, and Barry along with the rookies would be transported by my tree to their respective portal locations around the world. The trees and plots we see before us will be provided at the precise moment they are needed by each usher.

We were shown how to massively spread the message using global communications satellites and the Internet to advertise the arrival.

All are invited to come.

Literally, in seconds, we saw the first message go viral Jon and I were told to post. The message was simple and prepared for us. *" Ye who are weary come. The question is answered."*

In full colorful glory, the of precise locations of each garden were shown. Following this, a streaming video of our loved ones' journeys through the tree on Saturday was presented.

My location will see the initial trickle of people. It won't take long before the masses will come. Its activity will explode the quickest.

Volunteers will step forward from all walks of life as others are ushered to the message.

Next, we were shown the other twenty six locations as thousands upon thousands of bright colorful lights beamed heavenly.

The numbers of people shown were unimaginable.

It was made known to Jon and me all will not come, but we shouldn't worry about this. It was as expected.

It was also presented to us every soul was to be held accountable for their lives. The punishment was a soul removed for eternity from the presence of our Creator. They and their souls will be denied Paradise for eternity, and this will be made known. It will be shown to those taking the climb. Their trip into the blackness without the light will seem endless… no light will appear within their darkness.

Before this is revealed, their climb will be filled with all the evil they have done and how it has affected others. They'll only see the ugliness mankind has inflicted on each other and Earth.

Their climb will be one of hopelessness and despair.

At this juncture, those who are to be denied entry will remain worthy of redemption. They have time to repent and be saved — even unto the last second. If not, they and their souls will dwell for eternity in the darkness as shown in their first climb with no light to follow.

When they return, they must truly seek redemption by asking for forgiveness from God. Without remorse, there'll be no forgiveness.

We were also shown problems will arise in many parts of the world. But they will end quickly as the righteous will far outnumber the evil and doubters.

Some sects and religious groups will never come, and Heaven will be lost for those who are ruled by evil or false gods.

In thunderous voice, at this instant, He made it known to us no man, woman, or child in the history of mankind has ever been destroyed by his hand or from his command.

Specifically, He related, "What loving father would harm his children?

"All are my children.

"Many have what follows wrong.

"Those who perish Godless in life will remain so into eternity. They've reaped what they have sewn... believe not, prosper not. Bad fruit remains bad fruit lest it be plucked from the tree and removed of the garden.

"Your fruits and labors are good, and you will succeed.

"Those who decide to come and those who do not are yet worthy of salvation and inclusion."

What we were shown and told next will shock our world to the core.

We came back into our bodies. The other team members had arrived before us and were seated, circling the three in deep discussion. For the time being, their questions were answered, but within an hour, another joint trip was to come.

As we walked towards the gang, Jon said, "Better plan for about three hundred and fifty or so tomorrow, and parking will be a nightmare. Maybe, our new police friends can lend a hand with traffic and security."

"Yep, I see rookies squeezing a ton of lemons in the near future," I said.

All Power Comes from Within

And the Lord God said, "The man has now become like one of us, knowing good and evil. He must not be allowed to reach out his hand and take also from the tree of life and eat, and live forever."

—Genesis 3:22 (niv)

We joined the team and slowly, entered the round robin discussion. Jon advised the group within the half hour they would embark on their second round of training, but until then, he encouraged the discussion to continue.

Some were ahead of their teammates as to their line of questioning and interpretations of what they had just experienced.

For the first time, it became obvious to me the Paradise phase of their first climb varied somewhat. Evidently, different experiences were common and personalized as to where the contact with their deceased loved ones occurred and what the immediate landscape surroundings were like.

This fascinated and excited me. I found great pleasure in the fact personalization of one's visual and spiritual perceptions of the hereafter occurred for each of us.

At this time, I commented on the relief I felt our loved ones would soon experience some of what we had been shown. All of the ex-military and ex-police among us were keenly familiar with my next comments.

All the years on the department, I had made it a point to keep what happened on the job with the job. For over twenty years, I made it a personal rule not to unduly worry my wife, Rose, or my daughter, Faye, with what happened on the streets. Consequently, my family acted as if they never worried about me. When pressed, Rose would always respond to friends and family she didn't worry about me at work. She was confident I could take care of myself.

This time it was different. We had seen what was ahead, and I wanted my family to be with me for comfort. I have been comforted for what is to come. They deserve no less. This was occurring tomorrow, and I could hardly wait.

Jon chimed in, "By the way, congratulations, guys, you have successfully completed the first phase of this recruit school, and you are elevated to veteran status immediately. After this next session, you will have earned your real ranks of lieutenant."

With this, the thick ice of seriousness was broken with robust guarded laughter.

At this juncture, Thomas raised his hand.

"Yes, Thomas, ask away," said Jon.

"You are aware I have diabetes, and I am not fluent in any other language. If we are to travel for this assignment and you place me in a strange city and country, I will be of no good at all. I'm almost blind with cataracts. I have diabetes and cannot speak a word of another language," Thomas rambled, repeating himself.

At this, Jon, Jim, Matt, Barry, and I burst into sidesplitting laughter. Barry roared uncontrollably for a solid minute or two.

I said to Jon, "You might as well get used to it now, and just tell doubting Thomas to stow it. He is wasting our time."

Jon was way too kind to answer so abruptly and he explained, "Thomas, take those archaic eyeglasses off. No wonder you can't see. Advise me what you see at the wood line to the far right of the field. No comments now, just do it. No, Thomas, your other right."

Thomas did so and informed, "A momma quail and her four hatchlings."

Jon added, "Can you tell me what you hear there?"

"I hear soft cooing sounds and a cricket chirping," he said.

"No, Thomas, take a look in the tree above where the quail are standing and cooing. This would be the sounds of the morning dove. Do you see it?" Jon said.

Amazed, Thomas sat down and remained silent after replying, "Yep."

I stated, "It is almost time men and ladies for the next leap — the largest trip of your lives. Ladies, do any of you have any questions at this time? You have been quiet."

Within a second, with a half smile, Janet asked, "Rod, what are the chances of suffering jet lag from leaping so quickly?"

"Less than zero. The brain chemicals, kicking in at one hundred miles per hour from your previous leap, are about to go bananas," I exclaimed.

We and He should have chosen more women.

Jon continued for me, "You will be informed in an entertaining fashion exactly what we have been called to... maybe with treats. You will receive your orders, assignments, and all pertinent paperwork at the end of the tutorial. It will explain all you have been gifted like the rush high you've been on since the climb. Well, you'll learn this and many other new things are now permanent features of you.

"Oh, in case I forget it, our families will not benefit from the extras we all share, but they will take the trip. Alone, to me, this is miracle enough.

"So, feel good, gang, and in my opinion, realize we are blessed among all mankind. We are like the anointed descendents of the tribe of Aaron or the modern temple priests. This sacred tree and land are, and the others like this will be, the modern traveling temples from which we will invite humanity to take its first look behind the curtain. If you've had any Bible school experience, you might recall this honor was originally granted to Moses and his brother Aaron who was the first high priest of the Old Testament.

"Also, this is a no tobacco zone for tomorrow's festivities. A tobacco use area will be designated as anywhere from the newly cut road back to the dirt road behind all the parked cars. But as for the tree and surrounding land, not one blade of grass or leaf is to be harmed in any way. Those are our orders."

Jon called us to our feet, and off we went under and up into the tree.

This stop was uniquely different from our previous entertaining session with popcorn and drink. We were seated in a cavernous dimly lit room behind a rather large all-in-one touch screen computer system. There was one for each of us.

Sitting in a semicircle allowed us a convenient view of what everyone was watching on their screens. Once we had become familiar with our surroundings, a voice came from the computer and said, "Hello, look in your mailbox." Next, a written message flashed across the screen, "Silence, please. Silence and please, click enter."

We did and a little ladybug with a sultry voice began to guide us down her tutorial maze. The maze was more like a bright horizontal worm hole, looking and feeling exactly like the soft white light section, taking us into Paradise. As we entered the whiteness through a cloudlike wall, she exited our screens.

The next instructor was Jim dressed as a young Dutch girl with pigtails. He appeared at the far end of the hole. This was hilarious. It was Jim's mug, but the rest of him was the little Dutch girl in Oktoberfest attire. Jim was not amused. We were, totally. Jim held a full-sized unlit cigar in his right hand.

The rest of us were inside the horizontal hole with Jim, but we were floating at a distance from him or her. Jim took a draw from his unlit cigar, exhaling blue billowing smoke in our direction.

As the smoke cleared, he stated in a girl's voice, "Who are you?" He pointed the tip of the cigar directly at us. One by one we floated in line towards Jim. The entire lining or wall of the hole burst into *Willie Wonka* type colors with scenes and sounds. A brief biography of each team member was shown as well as pictures of their immediate family. These videos surrounded us while we floated weightless like in outer space. Simultaneously, we were able to comprehend all the visions and communications. Our ups and a few of our downs were portrayed. On the whole, it was a most impressive group of people.

As these scenes ended, I appeared on the wall before the team. I was dressed in casual attire for the beach. Initially, the background was totally white while I walked across the wall. Then, there was scenery behind me. I was walking on the beach in Paradise. To my left, a boat appeared on the water. I climbed into the boat and raced away. It was unclear whether this was a fishing trip or a simple boat ride. In a wink, the seas became rough. I was seasick. With head hanging over the side of the boat, I exclaimed, "At no time tomorrow will intoxicating beverages be allowed at the picnic. Bottled water, lemonade, sweetened and unsweetened tea only." Thankfully, I was able to get the "only" out before heaving ho. In a puff, the scene was over.

Next, dressed in a jumpsuit, Janet was shown tumbling, floating head over heels through the hole. As she softly landed head first on a protruding cloud, she snapped to her feet, faced us, and said, "Here's what has changed for each of you." She sprawled full out on the cloud with arms and legs spread. At this time, a bright purple light entered the hole, traveling towards us and her outstretched body. The laser-looking light scanned her body up and down twice. When the light had gone out, she sprang to her feet.

From her jumpsuit pocket, she pulled an iPad. Touching a few places on the pad, she turned the device in our direction, enabling us to see its screen.

At this, Thomas complained he could not see the message.

Janet took an earplug from her pocket and attached it to the device.

The list there covered the wall lining, encircling us. It chronicled the physical and mental upgrades each of us had received. She called on Thomas to "stand please," and he did. She spoke briefly to him in several dialects each of which was instantly uploaded into his upgraded brain. Without a hitch, he was able to talk with her in each language.

Next, she ordered, "Kindly read aloud the fine print at the bottom of the pad as it appears." Thomas complied and slowly read, "Please, shut-up, Thomas, and sit back down on your cloud. You are wasting our time again. Thank you, Thomas."

I love Janet's sense of humor.

The other twenty of his class were highly impressed, laughing and loving the presentation as well. At the end of this, Janet left her iPad with its screen visible to us. A list of warnings appeared for each of us, explaining how and when these attributes were to be used.

Leisurely, Matt entered front and center of the horizontal hole. He was wearing a wild zoot suit, a large floppy-brimmed hat, and a huge pocket watch with attached biker chain. He said he had plenty of quality time for us. The watch's face was as large as one of the pillow seats within the hole. We saw all the timetables and deadlines for our immediate futures. Then, Matt trucked on down the hole.

Barry appeared next as a well-dressed college professor, standing behind a lecture podium. The rest of us were seated in cap and gown, apparently, at a Mercer University graduation ceremony, or at least it is what the banner said, floating behind Barry. I had never seen Barry dressed in a suit.

He began to speak. He reminded the new veterans about the picnic... pets are welcome to arrive early tomorrow, to bring lots of ice, to help squeeze the bushel or two of lemons with, rather for Rod, to bring sugar, artificial sweetener, make tea, sweetened and unsweetened, ice the bottled water down, and lastly, assist in the general setup and clean-up of the whole event.

Jon loved this segment, dealing with chores.

We were told by Barry to return to the site later on after we had driven our families home for a final joint ascension — before heading to our posts the following Sunday afternoon. He continued, "In two days, we will be transported to our own gardens around the world." After this, Barry said, "Congratulations, Class of 2013!" Hopping up, we tossed our caps to the heavens.

In a twinkle, the ladybug had returned, and with one of her legs pointed to the sudden blackness around us, she said, "Look up," and she was gone.

One of the females on our team shouted, "Sing, ladybug, sing," and the other women joined in the request, "Yes, give us a song."

The small ladybug popped back to us, and her body blushed from red to dark maroon. She said, "Here goes ladies and gentlemen. This is for you." She fluttered her transparent wings a couple of times, and she was off, flying above us with the blackness to her rear. Slowly, an unseen full orchestra began playing her music. She had a heavenly voice which sounded like a choir. Her score had a harmony which echoed and amplified the melody I had first heard, coming from the tree. The ladies swooned, and the guys were hypnotized as ladybug sang for us. Her song is well known, *When You Wish Upon a Star.* As she was ending it, she pointed to the stars which now filled the sky, singing one last line while flying away into the night.

There wasn't a dry eye in the place not even ladybug's as she flew away.

We clapped, stomped, and roared. Janet lit a cigarette lighter.

"Now, on with the show. Watch the sky," ladybug sang in tune from afar.

The stars began to fade. The room became a domed IMAX theater.

We were shown every phase of our departures to come this Sunday and all our locations were presented in detail.

We saw some of the problems which would arise from such a massive undertaking — a taste of the political and spiritual unrest, coming from the revelation. We watched these subside, and the masses were with us. The message was too powerful. Throughout the world, evil withdrew.

We witnessed each other operating our gardens as increasing numbers of people streamed in and out in perfect order.

We had many come to us early and often with the words, "I've been called."

A voice Jon and I recognized said only to us, "This is how you will determine those with good intentions to assist you from those slithering, hoping to gain influence in the garden. Turn no good shepherd away. Expect true believers to appear this Sunday. They all will be blessed in my house. You will cast the tempters and temptresses out in my name. They will be easily recognized by each of you."

With this, the twenty six of us were returned to the garden.

The new crew were handed their paperwork, and for the first time, they learned where they would serve. Not one among them, not even Thomas, raised a voice against their locations or duties to come.

After this, we departed until the next morning and the celebration at the garden.

Gathering Beneath the Tree

Since I lived so close, I thought I'd arrive really early and get started on the fencing around the tree, setting the tables and chairs, and posting the signs Rose had made designating the parking area and tobacco use and tobacco free zones.

Rose had inquired, "Where will the restrooms be?"

I drew a blank. Quipping under her breath, she said, "Men!"

I phoned Jon in a panic about the lack of restrooms. Chuckling he said, "Don't worry, it has been handled. Five portable restrooms were delivered early this morning and placed alongside the new road towards the wood line. Trash receptacles were also delivered by the same company. I had no idea who had arranged this until the driver said, 'These might help, courtesy of the cops down at the local precinct.' He does work in mysterious ways."

"Are you already there, Jon?"

"Yep," he said, enjoying the fact he had beaten me there again.

"You dirty dog, you," I responded. "Need more lemons" sprang into my head. We will stop by WalMart on the way for lemons.

Rose and Faye agreed to come early to help us out.

I was the last one to arrive — number twenty six, and it was only 10 AM. Ahead of me, there were seventy to a hundred people there. Team members, their families, and quite a few pets could be seen in the distance, playing with children.

138

Everything was in place, and I mean everything except our signs, of course.

It would seem police still have connections as a local Chick-fil-A donated gallons of fresh lemonade and sweetened and un-sweetened tea with all the accompaniments to go along with the three hundred Chick-fil-A sandwiches the local restaurant. It was a total surprise.

The celebration was in full form. It gave all of us ample time to meet and greet each other — our families and pets. While we sat around the tables and chatted about life in general, our children and pets played nearby.

The police arrived, the vital ones in uniform and ones not busy with their families. Counting the officers already there with families, who arrived early with food, chips, bread, and desserts in hand, there were around a hundred or more of them. The entire S.W.A.T. unit was there with their families.

We had a grand old time from the start. Old friends and familiar faces were all around the garden.

Outwardly, Jon did not seem to be lonely or feeling the pangs of his solitude. Where I went, I insisted Jon come with me, and before long, he was simply a member of my family to those I knew and loved.

Noon came as more guests arrived. The parking was horrible, but we had uniformed traffic officers on post up and down the roadways into the parking lot to the edge of the field. They made sure close parking was provided.

When all the food, desserts, condiments, necessary utensils, plates, cups, and napkins were spread out on the tables, they covered eight big tables. One of the them was dedicated solely to the Chick-fil-A workers who catered their foods to the crowd. When they had it ready to go, their table was covered with a large Chick-fil-A tablecloth. They had brought the three hundred sand-wiches, keeping them warm in several big coolers. They also brought two large containers of coleslaw and carrot salad, packs of potato chips, plenty of tea with sugar and without, lemonade, and their usual dipping condiments.

We set them up with a couple of ample spaces between our tables and theirs. They would have three sides of their table from which to serve.

Our seven tables were lined-up end to end in a single file so the crowd could serve themselves from either side. Three and a half of our tables contained all the meats and main dishes. Two of them held the vegetables, dips, and crackers. The last table and a half which was actually at the front of the line held the desserts, breads, chips, dips for chips, pickles, salad dressings, and the necessary condiments, spices, plates, and all utensils needed. There were four new coolers filled beverages and three filled with crushed ice for the drinks. When all was ready, said, and done, the rookies had squeezed two bushels of lemons. Lemon slices floated in the two tubs of lemonade.

There was way too much food there.

All of fast food chicken restaurants were represented. The Colonel would have come in first if not for the Chick-fil-A table. There were tuna, beef, and chicken casseroles, sliced roast beef, country ham, slices of honey-glazed ham from one of the holiday stores, pulled turkey, slices of pork barbeque in buns with pickles, hamburgers and hot dogs in buns, a large tray of Swedish meatballs, a big tray of mild and hot buffalo wings from a local Hooter's (the Gwinnett police strike again) with celery stalks and plenty of blue cheese and ranch dressings for dipping, and more.

The vegetables also ran the gamut — cold salads, tossed salads with several types present, a couple of congealed salad rings, tuna and chicken salads, warm potato salads (southern and German styles), green beans, fried okra, creamed southern corn, boiled corn on the cob, southern fried green tomatoes fried the correct way (lightly-floured circular slices fried to a golden brown), sweet peas, lima beans, speckled butter beans, pole beans, baked beans, pinto beans, homemade cornbread dressing (Rose's mother's awesome recipe), Thomas's favorite food, stuffed deviled eggs, pickles, sliced tomatoes, celery stalks, iceberg lettuce wedges, and sliced and chopped onions.

Last but certainly not the least represented on the meats table, Pops brought gumbo. You read correctly. It is true. He brought gumbo to a picnic.

The dessert, chips, and bread table was filled to its edges.

The desserts were heavenly... pies of sweet potato, bean, apple, cherry, fried apple turnovers, mixed fruit, and blackberry. We had cakes for days — chocolate, coconut, yellow, devil's food with white icing (my favorite), pound, and even an early season fruit cake (actually, it was well received and Jon's favorite), brownies, strawberry and whipped cream pie and lastly, Faye's favorite, a chilled chocolate dream pie.

The breads and chips were varied. Thomas did fine. He had plenty of chips for the affair. I am telling you these folks knew how to cook... southern style which at minimum indicates a stick of real butter and pure cane sugar in everything, calling for such ingredients, that is.

We had not planned as well as we had initially thought. The police officers were represented in greater numbers than we'd anticipated.

But not to worry. We could have used more tables and chairs. Janet suggested we invite the kids, young adults, and anyone else who wanted to join her and a few of her fellow team members to dine on the lush green grass in true picnic style. This became an instant hit, and some of the adults joined the grass gang. In a snap, before the lunch bell was rung, the problem was solved by Janet.

Things had come together sooner and easier than anticipated. We had a few minutes more to relax, getting to know each other a little better.

A short distance from the tables, I saw Janet, sitting and talking with her fellow female ushers. I decided to walk on over, hoping they would allow a little male company into their circle.

I walked up and asked.

"Rod, certainly, join the powwow," Janet answered.

For a little while, their conversation continued as if I were not there. Janet decided it was time to turn the focus on me.

"Did you ladies know Rod and I graduated from the same high school in 1970? Rod played sports, and I was a cheerleader way back when. As I recall, he was a fair football player," she said while giggling.

I responded, "Yep, we sure did. Yes, I did. Yep, she was one. Yes, I suppose so."

I thought, "I know where this is going." I could feel my cheeks getting redder by the second.

Janet continued, "Did you ladies also know Rod and I dated a couple, well, a few times towards the end of our senior year? At the time, I'd broken up with the love of my life? During this period, my ex was off to college a year before me. Calling it quits made perfect sense to one of us. Any guesses who?

"So, I and old Rod here went out a bit. Do you remember this, Rod? Can you tell me the first time we hooked up? Girls, hooking up back then was strictly a kiss, hug, hug, and kiss thing. Tell me where we were at the time and what were we doing?"

Women remember everything.

Blushing profusely didn't go unnoticed by any of the six ladies, and I knew Janet had intended this. But it was all in fun for them and her... I rationalized.

I tried to be cool, responding meekly while looking skyward, "It wasn't too long after both of us had been clear of a boy or girlfriend. At the time, my latest one had dumped me.

"So, I'd say it was during our senior year when we went on a senior trip to Lake Lanier, skipping a school day. We rode there in the back seat, hugging due to two others squeezed beside us in

Bob's blue Ford. During the drive, I was flabbergasted you'd hug me period... even if we were pressed into it.

"The water was colder than hell frozen over, but we had our suits with us. We were determined to swim or at minimum, get wet. Everyone in the party of boys and girls clowned around a tad for a while.

"You stepped on a piece of glass, cut metal, or sharp rock, cutting your foot rather badly as it turned out. When you cut it and screamed, I was the first to swim to you.

"I remember picking you up in the water which was just below my chin. I cradled you, held you close, and looked at your foot. It was bleeding in streams. I was worried for you.

"I was carrying you to the bank, and in tears, you kissed me. You kept it up with me trying to make it to the shallow end as fast as possible. I was kissing you with one eye opened, looking for the bank. We washed your wound off with clean water we had brought with us.

"Someone in the group may have poured some of the liquor we had on the deep long cut. Your wound was wrapped tightly to stop the bleeding, and we loaded everybody in the car. You and I headed to the back seat. I held you in my lap all the way home to Atlanta, hugging and kissing the entire way back. It was a dream come true for me.

"Secretly, I had liked you since we were in Mrs. Wilkins' fourth grade class at Benteen Elementary. I used to come visit you at your house on the federal pen property. It was hurtful to see you with your boyfriend, but I was happy for you at the same time. I liked both of you.

"You are hands down the absolute best kisser and hugger I've known. Ladies, if you get the chance, you will see what I mean." After this comment, Janet blushed and slapped my arm.

"I don't recall whether you had stitches or not, but the cut was deep, wide, and long enough for them," I added.

Janet and the others feigned swooning with "Ahh, you're so cute," coming from a couple of them.

For me, it was fact.

Janet responded, "Not so fast there, Rod baby. This was not the first time. You forgot about the night several of us went to Stone Mountain. We had matched up like we used to do instead of outright dating. For the night, we doubled, and it was only eight days, an hour, and thirty minutes since I had broken up with your friend.

"I was still in serious mourning, and you knew it. You never realized this, but I and more than a few of my fellow cheerleaders knew you were a big teddy bear — the guy we most liked as a big brother — someone we could confide in the easiest. (I didn't say it, but I knew about this just friends curse, haunting me then and to this day).

"Well, after dark, we went to climb Stone Mountain. Bob was driving as usual. He and you had a quart jar of moonshine, as I recall. Before we started to climb the mountain, we sat in the back seat for a long time while Bob and his 'date' waited on us outside the car, sitting on an immense granite rock.

"I cried a lot, and you were embarrassed just like now. I knew you were really shy, a little scared, and hesitant since your friend and I had dated for a long time. I hugged you and finally, at first, you kissed me on the cheeks. This led to lips touching, kissing.

"Bob was getting anxious to get up the mountain, and I suppose he was tired of sipping moonshine alone. A few times, he yelled for us to come on. So, we exited and began the climb. You and Bob didn't make it halfway up the mountain or even to the bottom of the quart jar until it was time to head down. This was the first time we went out on an informal date situation."

Grinning, I answered, "Yes, you're right. It was a quart of moonshine — Apple Jack, I believe."

"Rod, we will not tell the girls about what you did to me on our infamous formal date after you'd gone away to Mercer University in Macon. I was in Atlanta attending Nursing School at Grady Hospital, and you had come home on break," she quipped.

After her statement, I stood to walk away. The guilt of what I had done to her this night remains like a thorn on my conscience. I apologized profusely afterwards to no avail. Janet never forgave me, and I don't blame her. I was an idiot.

"Tell, tell," a couple of the ladies stated.

Janet replied, "That's alright girls, we've had plenty of fun with him for one sitting. We have all the time in the world."

I heard her words, walking away, smiling at this reprieve from the gallows. I thought, "She was the best kisser and hugger I have ever known. Her lips were as smooth as velvet and as soft as a baby's cheeks. When she hugged you, her entire body conformed to yours like a new leather glove. Her hugs were sensual. Why do we have women on the teams?"

At noon, we called everyone together at the tables, and I welcomed them, introducing myself. I introduced Jon as my senior. This received lots of laughs. I turned the greetings over to Jon.

"I hope you all are as hungry as the children, and I can assure you we will have fun today. It is a glorious day here in the lap of God. He looked around the land and towards the tree. We want you to know this is a special place, and we've been cautioned to treat it as such. I will do so, and I know you will. We apologize for restricting any activity near, on, or up the tree for this event. For insurance purposes and to respect the wishes of the tree, as you can see, we have fenced it off," Jon informed.

Laughter rolled through the crowd at around three hundred and thirty by now. Some of the children even laughed at this or at the laughing adults.

Jon continued, "I think there is plenty to eat and drink for everyone. I see Thomas and Pops thought of the pets and provided a large bag of dog food and some dog biscuits.

"There are a good number of trash receptacles around, and if you didn't notice the line of bright blue potties located near the

145

dirt road, then, you, like Thomas, are in need of glasses. Please, feel free to use them when necessary.

"Some of you may not have heard about what a few groups have donated to make this wonderful picnic possible. Two of them did so for us on a moment's notice. Let's show our friends at Chick-fil-A and the county police officers our appreciation for their contributions. How about a round of applause for them?"

The crowd responded, clapping and whistling.

Jon added, "The youngsters who delivered and catered the Chick-fil-A treats have asked to stay and they were given permission to do so by their store manager."

Jon clapped again, and the entire crowd joined in. The men and women in and out of uniform were present at this.

"Well, we also have a surprise for you. After we've eaten and taken a few minutes to chat, loosening our belts and resting, we invite all present to visit and climb our tree. As you'll see and feel, our tree is unique. It'll be a life changing adventure for everyone. We'll climb the tree family by family or group by group.

"Officers, you and your families will join me and Rod's family members last.

"Everyone will be informed when your family will go, and one by one the other team leaders standing to my left will usher their family members for the miracle," Jon stated.

A soft rumble came from the crowd.

"Trust me, your feet will remain on the ground the entire climb. I assure you our tree is special," Jon explained.

With this, someone at the rear of the crowd shouted, "Enough talk. Let us eat. There's gumbo waiting." Jim was my suspect.

Jon replied, "Right you are, Jim. Please lower your heads for a brief prayer. Thomas, will you lead us in prayer?"

Without hesitation, Thomas began, "Lord, thank you for all of your wonders. Thank you for family and friends. Thank you for this day, your field, your tree, and this bounty for our bodies. May we journey to your house for another feast some day. Amen."

"Amen," repeated the crowd.

"Let's eat," I said.

One and All into the Tree

The meal lasted a little longer than usual. People ate at a leisurely pace with plenty of chatting along the way. After about an hour, it was apparent everyone was finished, except for a few children, enjoying their desserts.

I called the team together, and we decided to take the groups as the assignment lists had been given to the three. Jim and his seven with all their families would go first. The rest of the group would be advised to watch the tree for any signs when families walked beneath its branches. Barry and his seven were next. Third, Matt and his group would climb. Jon and my family plus the officers, their families, and the workers of Chick-fil-A would go last.

When all were finished eating, Jon called us to the tree. The crowd was told how this would happen, and they might want to circle the tree outside of the tree line some to have the second best seats in the house for the fireworks. At this, the children clapped wildly. Everyone did as directed.

Throughout the crowd, looks of uncertainty could be seen and especially, with the officers. But they waited and watched while the first group we're asked to head towards the tree.

Jim's family went first. While they walked, gathering beneath the tree, he advised them to look down at the ground until he told them to look up. He suggested they form a circle around the trunk. They had the numbers to do this. Each group would appear to have enough people to do so.

Jim repeated, "Clasp your partner's hand on each side of you, and when this is done, I will say look up. We'll do this together. Okay?"

"Okay," they shouted. Many of them were giggling nervously.

"Ready? Clasp hands. Shout 'ready' when you have done so," Jim instructed.

"Ready." circled the tree back to Jim, and he shouted, "Now, look up."

They did, and off they went in spirit... all of them at once. The tree lit up like a million balls of exploding fireworks at a dozen combined Fourth of July shows. Lights bounced in the hundreds here, there, and everywhere — in, around, up, down, sideways, in groups, and singles within the branches. In a wink, a beam in every color imaginable, seeming as wide as the body of Air Force One, rocketed to the heavens. The beam pulsated with life.

Viewing this, the onlookers were speechless. This display of beauty appeared to last about thirty minutes. When the beam fell back down into the tree, the family members below showed signs of movement.

Many cried, some fainted, and a few of the men had to sit on the grass beneath the tree. Several roared in pleasure, and a few stood stoic... as if frozen from what had occurred.

After a minute or so, I advised Jim to gather his family and move over to the grassy knoll to the west of the tree where they could sit or recline — a perfect place to watch the next group take flight.

I had to assure the crowd no one would be harmed, and I and my other team members have done this many times. This appeared to help calm them.

Barry and his group followed with the same instructions, but they stood clasping hands in circles grouped together beneath the branches of the tree.

They looked heavenly through the tree and swoosh. Their inner beings departed with the same visual displays. What a magnificent sight! Like Swiss clockwork they were back, and many in Barry's group fell to the ground in tears. Men stood there in reverent silence. The younger children went wild, watching the events from the outside. It was a laser light show and huge pinball arcade within a tree for them.

As Barry's group reentered their bodies, Rose grew closer, pinching me hard under my right arm.

"Ouch!" I responded, rubbing the spot of the pinch.

Over the years, I'd felt her pinch more times than I'd like to admit. This was Rose's usual reaction inflicted upon my under-arm flab at her moments of greatest concern, fear, or anger.

It was my official Rose alert to do something fast.

I rubbed harder and said, "Honey, just wait. I won't let any-thing bad happen to you or Faye. You know this. This is good. It's the best and purest good ever."

Matt's family was next, and off they went up into the tree and beyond. The fireworks were even more spectacular. Matt's group was the largest of the four. The lights imploded, and they were back without physically going anywhere.

Similar reactions like the others came from this group. The kids exploded into joyful celebration, and this was an amazing sight to see. Several ladies wanted to remain there in silence. They were led with tender force away to the grassy knoll. Upon exiting, three from this group lost their meals. Thankfully, it occurred in an area behind the tree.

Next, it was our turn to fly with Jon, the officers, our families, and the young workers from the restaurant.

As expected, the officers were suspicious. Their S.W.A.T. leader said, "Captain Travis, are you certain we want to do this?"

At which, I replied with a robust smile, "Captain, trust me and have a little faith. This is the ride of a lifetime, and it is not shabby at all."

They entered with us. My group clasped hands. Liftoff!

This time, I was able to experience the trip with my family beside me, holding hands as we bounced all over the tree, up, down, round and round, over here, and over there, pinging and ponging to the tiptop of our portal to Heaven and eventually, back.

I'd noticed the beam of light pass through Rose and Faye as it had me. I cried, believing I knew what the miraculous ray of light might mean.

We were headed through the universe with all of history and our life histories behind.

It was marvelous and better this time. I was with those I loved most.

Faye never stopped talking. She was having a ball, and like usual, she had to report to me and her mom blow by blow what was happening — as if we were not holding her hands and right there with her.

In tears, Rose watched in complete silence.

We entered the darkness, but it lasted briefly this go around. We flew into the light and out. Heaven was dead ahead.

Flying over it all, we saw the ocean, beach, sugary sand, and pastoral beauty near and far.

In the far horizon, we could see a huge palatial mansion. It would make the Taj Mahal look like a used playhouse. The closer we flew to it, the larger it grew.

In a wink, we were standing in a great hall with gold draperies. They each must have been seventy feet high and ten feet wide. As best I could tell, there were at least eight draperies — four of them on each side of the two huge parallel walls of the hall. We were here alone.

Within seconds, the massive doors behind us opened and in walked every member of both of our families who had passed. Previously unknown family members were made known to us... despite the fact we didn't recognize or know them.

My mother-in-law was holding a baby, and she let Rose, Faye, and me "hear" her thoughts. This was our unborn son... the boy we had lost years ago during a miscarriage. It was Rose's first pregnancy. She took the child in her arms. Tears of joy ran down our faces like never before.

Rose handed Faye our son and said, "Here, Faye, hold your brother." He was perfect. There was great jubilation. It was a true homecoming.

In our thoughts, a voice I recognized spoke softly to Rose, Faye, and me. The male voice said, "Fear not mother, father, and children you all will reside here in my palace one day. I have gone back on my word again."

"Thank you, Father," I said.

When His last word was thought, we were back under the tree.

Once we were all able to walk, we too sat on the cool green grass just beyond the tree's canopy. There were some three hundred and thirty people still here, laying and sitting on the grass. Not one spoken word was heard, crying could still be heard — Rose and Faye included.

We stayed there for a while. Afterwards, Jon and I stood and addressed the crowd. Certain conditions had to be met.

"Please, please, folks, tell no one about this experience. The time will soon come when the world will know and experience what you have witnessed here today.

"After the global announcement commences, feel free to witness to any and all who will listen.

"The chosen leaders here will be called upon for this mission throughout the world. Thank you all for your sacrifices. Times will be hard for most of you, but think back on what you just experienced. Everything is going to be alright.

"We ask each of you to leave this afternoon with peace of mind and soul. We will leave you shortly. Go home. Talk about this with each other. Compare your experiences and know they were real. We are blessed among all peoples," Jon stated.

The large majority of the people stayed for a while, mingling and chatting with each other about the wonders they'd been shown.

Briefly, Rose and I talked with Jim, Barry, and Matt — mainly about the good old days at Mercer and on the job. She knew Jim more than the others, seeing how we'd worked and played together for over thirty years.

Back in 1972, Rose had met Barry and Matt through me. They had become instant friends, and we four were together often over

the next five or so years at fraternity related events, parties, wed-
dings, and funerals.

Rose was always at ease with my friends, family, and cowork-
ers. She had the knack of making others feel at home and at ease
around her.

She always said she treated all of my male friends and brothers
like they were her brothers. She was raised with two brothers, one
older and one younger. Consequently, Rose could handle herself
around boys and men. The things she would say to my friends on
occasion would even startle me.

Rose was blunt and always to the point. She never minced words.
She blasted my pals just like her brothers when they got the least
bit out of line. They called her, Momma Rose.

I think Barry and I appreciated her candor the most. Jim and
Matt were often in her doghouse but especially, Jim. I tended to
also be there with some frequency.

When he saw a familiar police officer, Jim excused himself. He
wanted to speak with her before he and his family departed.

Barry and Matt decided to see if the Chick-fil-A gang had any
sandwiches left, and they hurried off.

At this point, Rose cut her eyes at me and under her breath,
said, "Earlier, I saw you over there with your old girlfriend. You
could've warned me an ex flame was one of your team members."

I realized my response would be tendered from the doghouse,
and I had to choose my words carefully or else the smaller house
address would be prolonged.

I responded methodically, slowly, "Honey, you know I could
tell you nothing about this whole affair. I meant to say this entire
mission until today. If not, you would have known she was on the
team sooner. In fact, and it is a fact, you can verify with Jon if you
like, I was as shocked as you to see her here and on the list.

"These lists of the rookies, of which she is one, were mainly
provided to us and not by us. I was able to pick some, but she was
not my pick. I didn't even know her married name which she still

uses — after the death of her husband three years ago."
By this point, it dawned on me I was stammering and not helping my case at all.

"Anyway, she wasn't my girlfriend back then or now. I only
went out with her a few times after she broke it off with Stan.
You remember Stan, don't you?

"I see Janet sitting alone over there. Let's go over, and I'll rein-
troduce you to her. You have already met and talked with her back
during the last RHS reunion — years ago, but let's go over."

Rose and I strolled over to Janet. She was sitting alone on a
knoll. We sat down beside her. I let Rose sit next to her, and I sat
with Rose between us.

It was plain to see Janet was pleasantly trapped in the tree,
visually and mentally. I hated to interrupt her meditation, but I
needed a hand to escape. After I cleared my throat for the second
time, Janet was back.

"Oh, I'm sorry. Hi, Rose and Rod. I was lost there for a few
minutes. You know, this is a marvelous tree. What's up, guys?"
she stated.

"Nothing. I wanted to introduce you to my wife, Rose, but I
think you've already met a least once back during the reunion.
At any rate, Janet, this is my wife, Rose. Rose, this is my dear
friend, Janet," I said.

In unison, they giggled and said, "Hello, nice to meet you
again."

"Hah, hah," I said, turning the grassy knoll over to them to
chat.

I reclined against the rise of the knoll, discovering a piece
of steak-o-lean I had first chewed at the end of the meal, tucked
between my back teeth and cheek. A good fried piece of tough
thick fatback, as it is often called, can last for days like a good
wad of gum — if you wanted it to.

Relaxing, I gazed toward the tree, as *Barney Fife* sprang into
my mind with some sage *Mayberry* advice, *"Rod, you got to nip
it, nip it... nip it in the bud!"*

The ladies laughed and giggled and as usual, mostly at my expense. Janet was actually kinder towards me than I had expected.

She told Rose about her husband, his passing and their grown children. They were adopted.

They talked about Faye, pets, and shared stories about mutual friends or acquaintances.

They were having a ball, and my future looked brighter.

Rose asked her if she ever thought to get remarried or if she dated after her husband's death.

She answered she was never interested in marriage again, and she had tried a date or two but added, "These days, all older men want younger women."

At this, Rose laughed and added, "Yep, these old frisky geezers wouldn't know what to do with a young woman anyway."

My ears started to burn a little.

Rose told Janet she was still young and attractive with a nice figure... and she should get back in the game.

At which, Janet replied, "What if Rod were gone, would you take your own advice?"

Cringing at the thought, Rose said, "No, I don't think so. I'm way too old and tired for such tomfoolery."

They and I chuckled.

Janet said, "By the way, I'd like to know more about the handsome guy you and Rod were talking with before you joined me. I know he is a team leader, but we haven't had much time for meet and greet around here. Things have been quite hectic. I would be interested in him. He's a looker."

Rose went bonkers, laughing so hard and rolling around so much, I had to sit up and see what was happening.

Rose took great pleasure in what she was about to say. She responded, "I assume you mean Jim, the thinner of the group with graying black hair — more graying than black these days. Well, I will do you a huge favor and not introduce you to him or even remotely suggest you get to know him better. But if your middle name is Sue, I may." Rose continued laughing.

Janet said, "I don't get it."

I said, "Rose, be careful there," as if she'd ever listened to me about such matters.

Rose replied, "He's single and about eight years older than you and Rod. At the beginning, he usually calls every female he comes to know Sue. It would be too difficult to remember all their names or something. It is a shame, but often, since meeting him through Rod, I've been called Rose Sue or plain Sue for years by him.

"Now, if it were me, I'd be chasing Jon."

For plenty of reasons, hearing this pleased me.

Rose dropped it there. She could see I was becoming upset with her, and I didn't have a pinch alert for Rose.

Janet responded, "Oh, now, I see it. Jon is also handsome."

Rose and I excused ourselves and joined the group nearest the bench.

Before the crowd dwindled, as was foretold, many had made themselves known to Jon, me, and the other members who had since been told of the instructions from the boss. Those with the comment, "I've been called" will assist us, starting tomorrow and with me here during the first days.

My site will be the busiest the fastest.

Many in the crowd assisted until everything was cleaned and the area was policed... to be around the tree a little longer. It has a hypnotizing allure.

The portable toilets, tables, chairs, and trash receptacles were taken away.

When all was done, not one blade of grass or leaf from our tree was in any way bothered. The complete area looked as pristine as the day He created it.

Team members were advised to see their family members home and immediately return.

Except for Jon and me, the garden was empty, and the burden of what was to come weighed heavy on me.

As a police officer, I had delivered the worst of news before to families, and it was one of the toughest things in the world to have to do.

In a few short minutes, Jon and I would face the most difficult task either of his has been called upon to perform.

Duty calls again.

We'd agreed this responsibility should be lifted from us. We were growing weaker by the minute, and the dread we shared had opened the door of temptation. Evil is persistent.

As we rested on the carpet of the garden, a peaceful sleep fell upon us. Temporarily, the devil's access was denied.

After a short nap, the respite was over. Our bench beckoned, and we took our seats, gazing in awe at the miracle before us.

Answers Breed More Questions

(Mary) said, "I saw the Lord in a vision and I said to him, 'Lord, I saw you today in a vision.'" He answered and said to me: "Blessed are you, that you did not waver at the sight of me. For where the mind is, there is the treasure." I said to him, "So now, Lord, does a person who sees a vision see it <through> the soul <or> through the spirit?"

—Gospel of Mary 8 (Berlin Codex; Berolinensis 8502)

J on and I rested leisurely on our bench after the last of the picnic crowd had left. It dawned on me we were simply two old coots wasting time on a comfy bench like many of the elderly across the globe.

The team would return for a final joint session before the next afternoon kick off.

Once we'd cleared the clouds of worry, this small window of spare time was a blessing. Neither of us was in a hurry to jump to the next phase, and apparently, neither Jon nor I had the energy or desire to play with any of our upgraded toys. The good old days of normalcy suited the moment.

My mind would not stop. I tried to find a power cord to unplug. I hoped Jon was resting more than this. Things were moving at such a fast pace. We didn't have the time or leisure to kick back and just relax, clearing our minds of an apparent impending doom.

"Kick off Saturday" flashed in my mind, and for the first time in weeks, football entered my thoughts. After all, we were in prime college and pro football season. This had been my favorite month throughout my life — October, a time of football and trick or treat.

So, I hit the power switch on my search engine, checking what college games were on the tube today, Saturday. The late afternoon games should be going. The USC Trojans were on. Yuck. Suddenly, I felt guilty for wasting this precious time on the old normal. Sports seemed trite now, and October's luster was gone.

During a heavenly gaze, I found it odd there are twelve months in a year, twelve disciples who followed His son, twelve tribes of the Jewish people, our picnic began at twelve, and twelve eggs to a carton. For some reason, the Tribe of Levi came to mind. In a small way, we were like them. I felt pity for the Levites and their descendants. Some orders are much more difficult to follow than others.

In my heart, I had always believed there were really thirteen followers of Jesus with Mary being first among them. I believe it was an abomination unto our Lord what the organized church had done with malice and intent to Mary Magdalene, assassinating her character.

If it had happened in these days, Mary would have sued those lying guys blind. All they did was apologize for making her into a prostitute when she was no such thing. It would be harsh even today. Mary was the best and I bet hippest apostle. I'd think she also loved October. Jon might agree.

If I get the chance to sit before the Man again before we hit the go switch, I might ask Him about all of this. Surely, he will answer my questions in some way... maybe, cryptically or in a general fashion. Either way would be fine with me.

I have read all the books of the Apocrypha, and it became obvious why these books and papers were excluded from the accepted canon we know as the Bible today. But on the whole, they were extremely interesting.

Josephus The Essential Writings was also interesting. In his writings, Jesus was briefly mentioned two or three times. If he were alive today not many folks would like Josephus. He wasn't one to "hitch your wagon to" as the cowboys used to say. To some, he was considered a traitor, of sorts, but I suppose he didn't have much of a choice. It looks like he could've foregone changing part of his name to a Roman one, Flavius Josephus. Once, I had a foot beat partner whom we called Josephus. At any rate, his history book was excellent — Flavius Josephus' and not my foot beat partner, Joe Josephus.

This brings me to the prophets. If given the right opportunity, I'll also ask Him about them. Throughout history, if not all, most prophets suffered greatly. They were killed in almost every horrific way imaginable. I recall the phrase "don't kill the messenger" came from their harsh endings in history. To be prophet was a high risk vocation then and possibly now.

We are sort of like the prophets of old, and I pray times have changed enough for us to be better received. The world remains a dangerous place.

It would also appear our Creator has changed greatly over time, or He's the same as He's always been. Maybe, it's been men who've flipped the script about Him. He's definitely in charge. He does have a sense of humor, and I never want to experience His wrath. As far as I know, He may well be a vengeful God. He has been anything but one to us. I like Him — or at least His voice and His actions.

I believe He has cured Faye and Rose. I will know for certain by tomorrow, but after the climb, Faye did say her back was feeling differently. She was standing more upright, indicating her spine had straightened some. She did report her pain was almost gone.

To me at least, medically, Rose also seemed different. During the picnic and climb, her asthma and allergies should have been going bonkers, but they weren't after it. Since the trip, I don't think she has used her inhaler once, and her sinuses seemed clear. We'll know in the morning, and if so, these are miracles.

For a few moments, I had completely forgotten what was to come, and it felt good. The impending doom flooded my mind.

Resting on the bench with his eyes closed, Jon said, "Rod, be quiet and get some rest. You're killing me. I can't help but hear and see what is going on in your head."

"What time is it anyway?" Jon added.

"Dude, really? Where is your watch? Have you ever worn a watch? Better yet, can't you access one with your brain or something? Danged, must I really look at *Mickey*. It is 1630 hours APD KRV 401," I said and grinned.

"Hah, hah, Rod, I know this means 4:30 PM, but what's the APD KRV 401 stuff? Did you forget how many armies I have served in?" Jon asked.

As cool as James Bond, I responded, "If I told you, I'd have to kill you... nah, it was the Atlanta Police Department's Federal Communications Commission identification numbers our radio dispatchers had to announce per FCC regulations. I suspect, you'll be expecting the secret handshake next."

"Yep, let me have it, and I'll wager you were restricted by the FCC from using profanity over the radio. Right, Rod?" Jon retorted.

We laughed.

"Oh, rats! Rod, we had a meeting planned with you know who at 4:15 PM. We're late. Why didn't you wake me?" Jon said.

"Not my fault, man. You knew this and not me, and by the way, have you noticed you sometimes tend to get hyper? Jon, you are four hundred and eighty years old," I responded, heading to His tree.

Ye Who Are Weary Come, the Question Is Answered

To the tree and zip, up we beamed.

Like usual, Jon and I were seated side by side but on a thick stack of Native American pony blankets before a big crackling campfire. In the dead of night, I could see a shadowy figure across the fire from us, but against a dark background, it was impossible to make out its features in the shadows.

I looked up, viewing a night sky filled with more stars than I had seen. An oversized harvest moon hung like a huge orange orb midway above the far horizon. I could almost touch it. To our left and right were massive mountains like those of Colorado or parts of the western United States desert. It reminded me a lot of the area where they have *The Burning Man* event out west each year.

Enjoying the fire on a crisp fall night, we sat on the warm sand of the desert or possibly, in a valley of the Grand Canyon.

From the far side of the fire, the voice came, "Good evening, Jon and Rod. I'm happy to see you made it."

"Rod, back there on your bench, you had a few good questions for me. You even brought up football. If we tarry long enough, a fine bench can evoke such inquiries. Well, this area has been my favorite bench site for hundreds of your years. One can relax here and allow the day's troubles to burn away, rising to the stars after dancing on the flames.

"Throughout the ages, man has gotten more wrong about me than right. You have tried, but consistently, you've misinterpreted the entirety of it.

"For instance, if I were a vengeful God, do you think I would allow the senseless slaughter of millions upon millions of my children? Down through the ages, this has gone on with mankind.

"Would I have allowed the indigenous peoples of America to be treated inhumanely, allowed concentration camps, gas chambers, atomic bombs, infanticide, ethnic cleansing, the unborn murdered, and on and on to occur without inflicting my wrath?

"Honestly, do you think I would tolerate slavery anywhere in the world, if I were as vengeful as some would have you think?

"No, those abominations are the creation of your fellow man. They were not inspired by me. These evil men didn't fear my wrath. Evidently, to this day, they don't.

"There have always been evil men and women among you, and they will always be with you. But their days are also numbered.

"Jon, you fought in the war, freeing the slaves in America. You saw the carnage, the inhumanity, and suffering. It almost killed a nation. This too was because of thick necked men and not me.

"You have controlled your own destinies, and I am with you always.

"The better question would be this. How could I have allowed such atrocities to occur without inflicting my wrath on man each and every time? If I were a vengeful God, you would have been stripped of free will.

"No. No! I am not vengeful.

"I am and have been sorely disappointed.

"What are your opinions about the tinker or clock maker theory? Did I wind up the universe and consequently, you and then leave? Rod, how long would your *Mickey* windup watch or a battery one like it last?

"These days, is it possible for man to be more in love with himself? Men, the last question is rhetorical.

"You'd like to know about miracles. Are they of my creation?

"Yes, there have been such moments.

"Miracles are performed and have been manifested with regu-larity. Mostly, they've been from the hands of extraordinary men and women — who may or may not have been inspired by me. But just the same, their miracles were real. I've performed a few myself.

"Why'd I send so many of my prophets to their horrible deaths?

"That wasn't totally on me either, but I claim responsibility.

"Evil is also eternal.

"So, add a huge doss of free will, a heaping cup of power, and a pound of good old narcissism in the mix and as the famous chef says, 'Bam.'

"When those who were sent by me to deliver the right mes-sage were destroyed, they were doing their jobs. Obviously, the delivery was given to the wrong leader at the wrong time and place. Any message I send by whatever means is the right instruc-tion to those in the greatest need for guidance.

"Evil men and women have stayed true to their natures. After, death they suffer in eternal darkness.

"My prophets are with me.

"You also have a job to do, one you will do. If anyone harms or causes harm to be inflicted upon any of you, payback will be — well, you know the rest of this one. Never forget, in the end, ven-geance is forever mine.

"The evil ones who now walk the Earth will be like blind rats forever scurrying in eternal blackness. This is my vengeance.

"Some people simply cannot and will not accept the truth. For example, look at Thomas in your group. If he were in charge and given the other ingredients mentioned above, I do believe a prophet would be about as safe reporting the weather forecast to him as an opposing croquet player in a match with the *Queen Of Hearts*.

"Was Mary an apostle?

"Here is a short and sweet answer, yes! You will meet her one day. Any who follow one of my messengers and contributes substantially to the furtherance of his or her works is an apostle. I have many prophets, many sons, and many apostles. In my house, they can be seen in numbers and soon, more will arrive.

"Can I save Earth? What can't I do?

"Should I save you? Do you deserve it?

"That which has been written will come to pass, and this has been written. When I say written, I do not mean in the rags there you call newspapers. There must be order somewhere in the universe.

"Some purported thinkers have theorized you never really die, but you are merely reborn after death on the same birth date as you have had throughout eternity, repeating the same life all over again into eternity. The true death is when you realize this and create your own eternity thus achieving Objective Consciousness. Poppycock! These concepts are not even close to the true meaning of Objective Consciousness, and totally, disregard fluff like the concept of Eternal Recurrence which is the crazed theory also of repeating your same life over and over for eternity or something similar. Sometimes, it gets so stupid I cannot keep up with the mountains of bull manure.

"For me, inform Barry he is full of tofu pudding, and he better flush out his headgear because he is a new guy. Rod, by the way, it is an order.

"Plenty of you think way too much and thus, way too little.

"The saddest and yet happiest being among us will be me on the date to come. All I have created there will be obliterated in mere seconds of your time. This date will live with me in infamy. But I will also rejoice in the knowledge your true beings, your souls will return here with me for all time.

"Your earthly lives are mere clothing. Naturally, the shedding of which is painful to you and yours, but they did get this one right. You should rejoice for eternity awaits, and verily, it is a million fold greater.

"My time is not like your time. Time and how it works in different planes has always been fascinating — even to me.

"The age of the universe is but mere hours for me. Have you ever wondered why when you are injected with a pain killer, anesthetized, or after applying the smallest dab of DMSO on a sore muscle the effects of which are introduced instantaneously and felt throughout your body? Immediately, these drugs travel your whole body while the needle is still inserted in your skin or the anesthesia inhaled. But you're so large in comparison to the volume of the drug being introduced into your system. Size is relative in this. For example, take a 'breath' as the event to be compared. In time, one breath of your Sun would equal all the breaths of Earth. It gets to be a dog year versus a human year thing... only on a much grander scale.

"Time from plane to plane is different. Can a round peg fit in a square whole? But they can both exist and be made of wood. Can they not?

"I love Einstein. He's one of the best souls. He never faltered, and he's with me. He had much of it right. He was also a fallible human being.

"Many there lament they cannot think like Albert, sing like Houston, paint like Monet, or box like Ali. These were God-given talents. So, don't feel too badly as all humans have talents, abilities, and opportunities... just not so readily discovered or utilized.

"Today, you have experiments in dark matter, cloning abilities, nana technology, and exploding works in genetics. Greater and greater powerful ways to eventually destroy your world are in the works and by the worst of nations.

"The theory of the feasibility to travel over huge distances by bending the fabric of space is promising for you, but to me, such distances are but a thought away. They're like a millennium of decades on *Mickey* or a trillion fold breaths of your Sun.

"As I said, my prophets have been many. As we speak, some walk Earth. For every true prophet, there are thousands of false ones. It has always been so.

"Rod, beware of Barry. Keep a close eye on him. He has the potential to play a modern day Judas role in your works. I fear he buys into a lot of the eternity is or can be personal mumbo jumbo. Neither you two nor any of mankind can create their personal eternities. It does not work this way. It is as simple and basic as it can be. There are only two paths my children can take, and it is each individual's choice.

"Due to free will, you will have earned your place. Only two ultimate destinations exist, only one destiny per soul and there are no multiple souled people... trash! Your souls will either be in the light with me in my place for eternity or fallen from grace in the absence of light forever. I am the light. Work towards one or the other. There is no third way or place.

"Those who do not believe in me or their eternal souls and believe at death will consciously receive what they believe. So, they are half right. Option number two will be fulfilled for them.

"The more rational option and the best one is to believe in me. Live a moral life, obey my commandments, and know you have a soul. Yes, your being will live forever with me. This has always sounded simple to me and a no brainer really. Think of it like this, what if you had one last dollar, and you had to bet it in Vegas. The final dollar gambled either won or lost. A win gives you Heaven. A loss means an eternity of darkness. Your odds are even. What would be the smart bet? In this game, the dollar is your soul. It's always wiser to bet to win.

"In my presence, the possibilities are endless, and in as much, personalization would appear to be a perfectly correct option. It is to a point, but nothing is possible if you haven't earned the right to be in my presence for eternity.

"In fact, this has never been made known to any of my children. In history, each and every one of the people who've been shown my presence by voice, form, or both could have easily remained with me, if they had truly wanted. A few have asked but not in earnest or with certainty. You two could have stayed here with me at our first contact or during any subsequent meeting.

"Back in the olden days, I brought a few straight here while alive. It was always a reward. Read your Old Testaments again. Jon and Rod, you could remain now, but I know you will not.

"Take heed, during his last hours, even my most beloved son asked me to take his burden from him. He also was shown and told what was to come. It was written.

"Having the knowledge of what is to come for you and your team is a necessity, and I admit it will be most cruel. He who gives his life for his fellow man becomes favored unto me for eternity. Here and now, you are willing to do the same for me. What do you think it means to me? I pick my prophets wisely.

"The real kicker is your presence here with me is like a hot magnet unto my being. It might sound trite, but I want you here with me more than you desire Paradise. You are my children.

"Rod, for example, I've seen what happened with your family and your father. Yet, you honor him still.

"Close supervision of Barry by both of you, please. If you need me on this, ask and I will come down... been a while... might be fun for a final time.

"Jon, you and Lucy, Rod, you and Rose, have lost a child prematurely. When you were shown your children, living here in Paradise, how happy were you? How intense were the currents within you to remain with them? Do you expect less of me?

"Men, I too am old and yet timeless, but I fear I am growing more weary by the millennia.

"This is and has been my favored park bench for ages.

"Things used to be handled differently, but change is also eternal. Thus, I have changed a bit as mankind has a lot.

"Not so long ago, my methods were much more radical. Major advances in technology have come so rapidly. My antiquated ways are... well, too old.

"Just maybe due to technology and man's ever expanding curiosity to know, you are growing too close to me. Probably, man is beginning to be too godlike.

"You have the knowledge and technology to clone a human. Possibly, this is a strong enough case alone to allow the plug to be pulled. Do you honestly think a cloned human would have a soul? There is no sharing of a soul on Earth.

"Rod, earlier today, I saw you pick up your Bible — the one Rose gifted you back in 1973 when you were first married. I know it is the first Bible you had ever owned, and you still have it. Well, I saw you had to clean the dust from it before you started thumbing through it this morning. I know you have read if often through the years at intervals, and I also know the Old Testament can tend to be drier than the desert here. But you have read it more than a few times. I also like the New Testament more and more.

"For too many years, it has been no secret my books have grown dusty. These days, there are simply too many distractions for my people. They have turned away from me by the millions, and like me, I believe you have seen the results.

"The whole 'God is dead' drivel didn't help either. Too many have come to believe it. I am the one God, the God of all, and the living God. But too many say and think I am dead. Take a hard look at Detroit, Chicago, the Middle East, North Korea, and most of the Dark Continent today. There are those of my children who think everyone must believe as they do or be killed. By whatever name called, I am the same. The entire slaughter of others in my name has never been my wishes for mankind. It is also a first class one way ticket to door number two — eternal darkness.

"Today, all over the globe, the young people show no inkling of turning these trends around.

"Professional football? Don't get me started. If they don't straighten up down there, I may have to put a pox on all their houses.

"I have enjoyed following your earthly sports forever, and I do love football. But at the same time, can either of you give me a rational explanation as to why they drummed one of my sons completely out of the game? I can fully appreciate the whole talent thing, but after all, these decades, it looks like someone in an owner's booth would know the value of the 'it' factor. The fine young man has it in spades. After all, it's only entertainment.

"Like no one else, Hollywood recognizes the it thing. Look at Monroe and many others who had it. But this football player was sent packing after a conspiracy of hate was directed at him, simply because of his spirituality. He was the true player with 'He Hate Me' sewn on the back of his jersey. Never have the press, talking heads, sportscasters, owners, and fellow players judged and executed another player so thoroughly without cause like this man. The people love him and especially, the ladies. If I had a single daughter, I'd want her to marry this guy. As a comparison, look at all the other players still playing on Sundays, Mondays, Thursdays, and so on who are lucky they aren't in jail... much less, booted from the game.

"The entire injury for bounty mess and the players' union junk should have rolled heads — figuratively speaking of course. Look at what happened with one head coach. I told a few close friends the owner would totally compensate him for this year's coming contract. He would be paid all the millions he'd lost during the suspension. Yep, as they say on the golf course, bingo, bango, bongo. I win again. Where's my pox box? Again, it is totally entertainment driven. Regardless, the league should never tolerate the intentional, possibly criminal, behavior of any player to hurt anyone in the game. Having a team bounty on such quasi-criminality is beyond the line, but what do I know.

"Like I said, don't get me started.

"I could continue, but I grow weary — and yet, reborn in spirit when I know we'll soon be together again in my house.

"Jon and Rod, your sixty-four million dollar question might be. Does he have the power to stop these things from happening?

"Yes. Yes, I do.

"But should I?

"What do you think?

"Do you have other questions?"

Jon looked at me and me at him. Mentally, we were exhausted.

"I have one or two additional questions or requests," I offered.

"Go ahead, Rod," He said.

I stated, "You said earlier on Earth there is only one soul per person? Is it or can it be different in Heaven? Are there others like us in the universe?"

He laughed and simply said, "Yes."

Prior to the any other questions, one or all of his questions seemed purely rhetorical. It was clear He would not expand on the last answer. Jon and I were as confused as ever. He can be an elusive and tricky deity.

"Sir, I have another question or a request?" I said.

Jon added, "May I ask one question, sir?"

"Men, don't call me sir. Call me I AM... no, just kidding... that part of the movie cracked me up... I do have a name you know... look it up on your eye Google or Bing thing.

"And I'm reminded by history, let Barry see what happened to a few of the men who betrayed me. Show him the Judas affair and ultimate results. The Judas one they got right, too. You don't take your own life and sit before me in my house. You have reaped the eternal darkness.

"I know this may sound a little hypocritical in light of some of my previous statements about staying here. It may be construed by you as a suicidal act. It is not. You'd be here at my express invitation. While alive, you'd be welcomed into my kingdom.

"Have you considered what happened to Lazarus after he was raised from the dead? They sort of let the follow up drop.

Well, he did not live forever. Shortly thereafter, he died again. He did die twice. If you choose to stay here today, you will have been raised while living, and this is a limited club in these parts — thus, no suicide.

"Show Barry from the Old Testament where I took Moses to the mountain for the final time, showing him the Promised Land he had desperately sought for over forty years. Emphasize the fact I denied him the satisfaction of setting one foot on it. He'd always defended his flock — no matter what they had done, during those forty years. I gave in to him way too many times. This got real old, real quick, and it did not please me. So, he was shown the Promised Land and advised for his constant defense attorney approaches, he would die before he crossed the river Jordan into the Promised Land. He is one of my most favored sons and with me always, but you can go to the watering hole only so many times. They also got this right. I used to be somewhat vengeful.

"Any parent knows there is nothing easy about dispensing tough love... not a thing.

"I'll take your question first, Jon. You look sad. What is troubling you, my son?" He stated, speaking softly.

Slowly and carefully, Jon responded, "I remain overwhelmed by the recent appearance of Lucy and my son, Patrick. Seeing them together as if alive has affected me more than anything else in my life. More than I would have anticipated. I am confused and excited at the same time. My question is coming, but for me at least, it is complicated. When I first bought the tree for seven small fish, basically, I was given immortality. I have not aged one day in four hundred and fifty years. I was thirty when I made my first climb, and I have remained thirty for centuries... at least outwardly.

"Lucy appeared to me as she looked before her death. In fact, she looked even younger and with an external beauty, I've not seen before. It was like her essence was perfect.

"Patrick was seen as an infant like he would have been if he had lived. Yet, he also appeared absolutely perfect.

"Frankly, when I first saw them, I thought they would have been older. I was a little shocked Patrick remained an infant.

"When our time comes and we are called home, will we be like Lucy and Patrick? Will Patrick be an infant for eternity? Will he, or better yet can he, age? Will we age in Paradise, or can we age in Paradise? Did I see Lucy and Patrick as they are or as I mentally, projected them to be? I am sorry for all the questions, but these are the things which cloud a muddled mind and burden an old heart."

God replied, "Jon, my oldest son, do not be confused or saddened. The answers you seek will raise you higher than my tree has thus far. Regardless of your age, you are shackled by a mortal's mentality.

"The *Mickey Mouse* watch Rod wears keeps time within a system having a definite beginning and ending. We are back at the whole time thing. When Earth is obliterated, the watches go with it.

"Look at it this way. Here, before these beautiful surroundings, time does not exist. Paradise has no time zone. Your time does not exist here.

"Lucy and Patrick will appear as you wish. Currently, you are clothed in the trappings of mortality. When you join Lucy and Patrick, all of you will be perfect. Your souls are perfect. When in Heaven, you will have the capability to be as you wish. Your soul is ageless — now and when you come home.

"You and Lucy may visualize yourselves at any age. Patrick is able to the same. You can see Patrick as he would be as an adult or Lucy as an infant.

"During your initial climb, think back when you were shown your conception. The entire process was a microscopic glimpse into the power of the soul... your soul. Everyone in Heaven is perfect. In Heaven, we appear as we are, and this is always perfect. You cannot begin to grasp what is to come. But trust in me, men, and you'll see.

"Your turn. Shoot, Rod," He stated.

I was afraid to ask now, but I asked anyway, "Will you show us now exactly what is to happen and when? Surely, we'll need your guidance in breaking the worst of the news to the team."

With this, He said, "Look up."

First, we saw scripture.

> But the day of the Lord will come like a thief, and then the heavens will pass away with a loud noise, and the elements will be dissolved with fire, and the earth and everything that is done on it will be disclosed. Since all these things are to be dissolved in this way, what sort of persons ought you to be in leading lives of holiness and godliness, waiting for and hastening the coming of the day of God, because of which the heavens will be set ablaze and dissolved, and the elements will melt with fire?
>
> —2 Peter 3:10-12 (*The New Revised Standard Version–*
> *Anglicized Edition*)

Next, a Wikipedia article on a Super Nova or Supernova was shown, starting with;

> A supernova (abbreviated SN, plural SNe after "super-novae") is a stellar explosion that is more energetic than a nova. It is pronounced or supernovas. Supernovae are extremely luminous and cause a burst of radiation that often briefly outshines an entire galaxy, before fading from view over several weeks or months. During this short interval a supernova can radiate as much energy as the Sun is expected to emit over its entire life span. The explosion expels much or all of a star's material at a velocity of up to 30,000 km/s (10% of the speed of light), driving a shock wave3] into the surrounding interstellar medium.

173

This shock wave sweeps up an expanding shell of gas and dust called a supernova remnant.

Nova means "new" in Latin, referring to what appears to be a bright new star shining in the celestial sphere; the prefix "super-" distinguishes supernovae from ordinary novae which are far less luminous. The word supernova was coined by Walter Baade and Fritz Zwicky in 1931.

Supernovae can be triggered in one of two ways: by the sudden re-ignition of nuclear fusion in a degenerate star; or by the collapse of the core of a massive star. A degenerate white dwarf may accumulate sufficient material from a companion, either through accretion or via a merger, to raise its core temperature, ignite carbon fusion, and trigger runaway nuclear fusion, completely disrupting the star. The core of a massive star may undergo sudden gravitational collapse, releasing gravitational potential energy that can create a supernova explosion.

Although no supernova has been observed in the Milky Way since SN 1604, supernovae remnants indicate that on average the event occurs about three times every century in the Milky Way. They play a significant role in enriching the interstellar medium with higher mass elements. Furthermore, the expanding shock waves from supernova explosions can trigger the formation of new stars.

—Wikipedia The Free Encyclopedia

Ending with;

Milky Way candidates[
edit source | editbeta]

Several large stars within the

Milky Way have been suggested as possible supernovae within the next million years. These include Rho

174

Cassiopeiae, Eta Carinae, RS Ophiuchi, U Scorpii, VY
Canis Majoris, Betelgeuse, Antares, and Spica. Many
Wolf–Rayet stars, such as Gamma Velorum, WR 104, and
those in the Quintuplet Cluster, are also considered possible precursor stars to a supernova explosion in the 'near'
future.

The nearest supernova candidate is

IK Pegasi (HR 8210), located at a distance of 150 light-
years. This closely orbiting binary star system consists of
a main sequence star and a white dwarf 31 million kilo-
metres apart. The dwarf has an estimated mass 1.15 times
that of the Sun. It is thought that several million years will
pass before the white dwarf can accrete the critical mass
required to become a Type Ia supernova.

—Wikipedia The Free Encyclopedia

Our Sun will reach critical mass on December 21, 2014 at
6:00 PM EST. Earth, as well as all planets closer to the Sun and
those beyond Earth possibly to include Saturn, will be obliterated
in mere seconds.

The news verifying this impending event will finally come from
scientists around the world after our repeat messages with demonstration of this event have been shown. Six months prior to the
annihilation event, Jon and I will broadcast it seven straight days
around the globe.

Around the world, the message will come and be played during
the eighth month of portal operations.

As it turns out, the real goal of the first global appearance and
operation of the portals from October 2013 to June 2014 will be
to put the people at total ease with this knowledge.

Starting in July 2014, the people of this planet will be advised
they have a choice to make. They can stay here and die with the
planet or take the portals and instantly, enter the hereafter. Our

writer in Heaven's desert flashed again in my head with the thought, "No purchase required. Take the ride. Climb the tree."

Regardless of which they chose, it meant an instant loss of this life form. Truly, there is time to repent and live forever in the light of God... until the last second of the last minute before utter destruction.

The portals will be up, manned, and running to the end of days.

The scientific community will learn they have dramatically miscalculated the age of our Sun by many millions of years. It has been in its final dying stages for several million years.

Next, above the fire, we saw the upcoming event played out for us on a dark starless sky. Also, we witnessed every portal in use as the Earth exploded in flames. Including Barry, we twenty and six will perish with our planet, manning our trees.

With the sky in flames, Jon and I were sent back to our bodies.

The twenty four had arrived, and this was to be our last formal meeting until we said our goodbyes the next day, Sunday. The mission was a go.

Jon welcomed them back and jumped right into the mission.

He advised, "After this evening, we will report back in the morning at 0900 hours for departure."

Earlier, I had been advised the apartments and other housing which had been procured in advance by him were actually intended for the immediate families. They were welcome to travel to their loved ones dwelling, living there at any time after the usher arrives on his or her location.

Personally, we would be required to man our sites for the next fifteen months without a break. We were not to worry. This would be explained to us once we were on site and active. Plenty of assistance will be given to us. A camper, trailer, or office shack would work nicely at every portal. We should not worry about any of this because it too will be provided.

At this point, Jon and I split up the group.

He took the rookies, and I had their three supervisors for further instructions.

Jon and his group used the time to chat and tell a few jokes. As often directed, I had the dubious honor to speak with Barry. After a couple of supervisory comments as to the logistics and ideas for optimum usage of resources, I asked Jim and Matt to go over with Jon's group. Out of view of the others, Barry and I took a walk to the other side of the tree.

Barry knew something was up, and he looked a little nervous.

"What's up, Rod? What did I do?" Barry said, fidgeting a bit.

"Barry, before tomorrow, we have to get some things straight. I am about an inch away from scratching you from this. I have to question your sincerity, beliefs, and motives for being here, and it is a difficult thing to admit. Through the years, we have had numerous conversations about life, death, and what might lie beyond. You're keenly astute in these areas and have studied many philosophies and religions. These traits are what brought you here at my request.

"If I allow you to stay and see it today, what you will be shown will not be easy. The last thing we need on this task is a Judas. Barry, are you our Judas? After all you have witnessed and been shown, will you take the opportunity to hijack this mission for your own good? In our group, will you become a false prophet?

"I will not tolerate this, and I have been told in the harshest of terms by our leader you will suffer as greatly as any in history who has gone against the voice. I hope you fully appreciate what I am telling you. Look at the tree, now."

With mouth agape, Barry gazed at the tree. Scenes throughout history were shown of those who had denied and went against God's wishes. He saw the plagues of Egypt and the Pharaoh's army drowning in the sea. He saw Moses denied the Promised Land by God for his defense against God's wishes for the evil done by his flock. He saw Judas betraying Christ and later, being

hanged by his own hand. He saw the thirty pieces of silver returned to the temple priest and the land bought with the same
blood money. To this day in Israel, it is a pauper's cemetery. He
saw Lucifer as an archangel and then, his betrayal of God. He
saw many of the false prophets and their souls trapped for eternity in the hell of darkness. Finally, it was over.

"Barry, do I need to send you packing? Or, will you promise us
you will not sabotage this operation? This is not about you or us,
my friend. This is infinitely larger than us. Can't you see this? You
have a choice to make. Comply and stay, or admit you're not worthy
and go.

"I do not want to hear Objective Consciousness, Eternal Transfer, or make your own eternity bull crap from you again. I certainly
don't want the people you are mandated to lead to hear this junk.
What's your answer?"

Barry was shocked and I think, a little embarrassed. He did
seem humbled, and meekly, he responded, "Rod, I am sorry I've
been or may still become a disappointment to everyone involved.
I am sorry you were called on the carpet because of me. You are
right about my thoughts and potential to preach another message,
if given this opportunity. Trust me. I have laid all of it to rest. I've
seen the proverbial light and path. It is the one path of truth and
right. It is with all of you and this mission. I wish to stay, and I
will prove to you I am a team player. All the other stuff is exactly
as you described it. In light of what we have been shown, I do believe."

"Great, this is all I wanted to hear. Let's join the others," I said.

Jon and I gathered the twenty four beneath the tree, and we
reclined under the canopy on the cool lush green grass. I love
October. In a new way, we looked upon the tree's branches. The
entire circumference of the canopy became a white movie screen
with one last message to be delivered before our departure.

This message was hosted by an aged Jon dressed in buckskin
frontiersman attire. He was standing on top of a huge mountain,

holding one of his cane fishing poles. Jon looked every day of four hundred and eighty years old. He had deep long wrinkles on his face, long white hair, and a flowing white and black-speckled beard. He was standing on a mountain which he advised was, "God's mountain." As we ascended the mountain trail closer to him, goats could be seen clinging to steep ledges. Below us, faint barking sounds could be heard. It sounded like a hunting dog had treed some quarry.

Jon took his cane pole and pointed it towards the blue cloud-less sky and said, "Watch." Instantly, twenty six large screens appeared, covering the sky.

With the use of all these screens, running simultaneously, we were shown our missions in the greatest detail to date. Our brains could easily handle the twenty six scenes as they played together but independently. Every aspect was shown and described. We saw what was to happen at each phase. How we were now engineered to forego sleep, rest, and even the necessity to eat and drink. If we desired, we could do them. The new no sleep trait will be needed when we start or tasks. We would never be tired again and never need to rest.

For some reason, I missed the garden bench.

With visuals, we saw how the world was given the messages from the first Sunday to the doomsday warnings. It was brilliant and yet, actually easy to access the world, using all the modern technology known to man plus God's extras. Around the globe, the sky became one giant movie screen when Jon or I needed to deliver His messages. All of the communication satellites around the globe were at our disposal.

Globally, we witnessed every problem as they occurred. We had thousands of followers, helping at each site. It was an amazing process to witness.

Miraculously, as shown to us, it only took about four months for the world to dramatically begin to change. At least, the people did in mass. The militaries, politicians, and governments were a lot slower to follow. Apparently, they had too much to lose.

Each family of the twenty four relocated to their loved one's city. Jon and I stayed closer to home. It was the beginning of a period of peace, non-materialistic prosperity, joy, and brotherly love. Many marvelous things were happening on our Earth.

Within six months, the majority of people had made the jump. Next, we saw the end, but beforehand, the mass rush to leave the planet. Then, there was quiet and calm. Millions upon millions left early... the sickly, aged, infirmed, and those with terminal illnesses. Many did so who were old or just weary. Many congregations and entire families exited together.

More people than you might imagine chose to ride the event out with us at the portals. In and of itself, to those who remained for whatever reason, the end became an inspirational celebration of life and our impending deaths. Truthfully, we rejoiced in the coming of the end.

Barry's site had the largest crowds, and they looked strangely like the parking lots during *The Grateful Dead* concerts back in the old days in Atlanta. I could smell the patchouli, freshly-baked hashish brownies, and the music was fantastic. Barry knew how to go out, and he remained true to his word.

Thomas's site had the most pets to take the climb with their human loved ones. Pops was jealous.

My family was with me up until the last seconds when they made the jump with our cat Percy.

I wished I could have been with Jon when it came, but at the end, we were chatting mind to mind.

The last words I heard from Jon were, "No way, dude!"

Beforehand, I had asked for a refund of my thousand dollars. Before he could fully field this question, it was over.

The show ended. We embraced each other and said our goodbyes until tomorrow.

Sunday came too quickly. I hugged Rose, Faye, and Percy our crazy cat, telling them I loved them, and I'd see them later.

As I walked out, I let Faye and Rose know how happy I was they were no longer suffering from pain or ailments. I went back in, hugging and kissing them again. It was a miracle.

I was weak and didn't want to leave.

Jon and I arrived first and immediately, broadcast the message worldwide in all languages. By all means available, the text message was delivered as given. It read, "Ye who are weary come... the question is answered." Streaming live video, depicting the locations of the portals, arriving with their keepers, was shown. Lastly, a video ran, showing all the picnic attendees from the day before, taking the journey with the tree in animated colorful glory.

After all, it made perfect sense to reveal this at this time. My site was the first to be used by the public, taking the climb. This message and visuals would play on the hour for the next twelve hours straight. The process was simple and phenomenal.

Go Time, No Turning Back

I am the good shepherd; I know my sheep and my sheep
know me – just as the Father knows me and I know the
Father – and I lay down my life for the sheep. I have other
sheep that are not of this sheep pen. I must bring them
also. They too will listen to my voice, and there shall be one
flock and one shepherd. The reason my Father loves me
is that I lay down my life — only to take it up again. No
one takes it from me, but I lay it down of my own accord.
I have authority to lay it down and authority to take it up
again. This command I received from my Father."

—John 10: 14–18 (niv)

The twenty four arrived a few minutes early.

Jon said he didn't think the Man would mind if we began early. So, with hugs all around, we wished each other luck and shook hands.

Barry stated he wanted to address the group before we departed.

I was a little surprised at this until I realized this was just like Barry. He had been one of the quietest team leaders throughout the past sixteen or so days. I had missed my friend Barry, the bubbly, talkative, and fun-loving extrovert. I felt badly for scolding him.

Maybe, in a manner of speaking, he had been reborn, and we were about to see and hear him as he used to be. After all, he is a brilliant man.

Now, Matt for example, had conducted himself as he always had. He remained cool, unflappable, and introverted.

Barry stated, "There has been something bothering me. No, bothering is not strong enough. It's more serious like a mother nagging at her teen son. When I first caught sight of this tree, Matt, Jon, Jim, and Rod will attest, it vexed me, I sensed this tree and area were much more than what meets the eye.

"During the revelation, something or someone made it clear to me I was on sacred ground. I declared our tree to be the vessel of everything sacred such as the Ark of the Covenant, Ten Commandments, the Holy Grail, the true Shroud of Jesus, the Tree of Knowledge, the Spear of Destiny, and infinitely more — in part, possibly, our Creator himself. At each step of the process, my thoughts have been reinforced. Briefly, Matt and I talked about this during the picnic. But, and this is a huge one, something remains stuck on pause in my mind... even with the many added goodies. Maybe, just a far outside the lines sort of maybe, it is even greater in importance than I suspect.

"Matt, you understand some of what I am suggesting here. I can see it on your face and in your actions. You are stroking your handlebar moustache like you do when an epiphany strikes. Matt, do you have anything to add or say on this?"

Matt, who has been the most silent team leader to date, said, "I hear you, brother, and I have been feeling some of the same vibes, man. For example, this portal, window, door, curtain, tree, or whatever you see it as is like a sum of everything in creation. It might possibly be too human, common, or crass to say this beautiful thing we are about to blastoff through makes the Hubble Telescope look like a Cracker Jacks magnifying glass.

"This said, I'm also in search of a few more answers. Jon, this question is for you, and it is an easy one of vital importance. Let me preface it some. Of all here, we know you have been with the tree and responsible for it the longest. In as much, you have had the greatest opportunity to use, study, and travel it. Here's the question. Have you ever been transported body and soul anywhere by the tree? I mean, in all your travels to prepare our way, were you ever allowed to use this tree as a transporter?"

Jon answered, "No. I have not, and I have never thought about it. But, as I have related, my initial seller did ascend through the tree to somewhere. I had assumed it was to Paradise. But was he called home body, mind, and soul? Yes is the obvious answer, and I expected to be treated in the same way when my job was completed. In fact, I never thought I would be here to meet anyone other than Rod, you, Barry, and Jim. In a clouded way, I sort of understand where this is headed."

I could see Jon was starting to comprehend much more than he let on. He knew what Barry and Matt were suggesting.

Matt continued, "I did not think you had. Rod, from all of your sessions up there, have you or Jon been shown where a living being was or had been transported anywhere at any time through this portal?

I replied, "No, while I was with or without Jon, I nor we have not." Now, I was beginning to see where Barry and Matt were taking us.

"I also knew your answer, Rod. Barry, rock on, my brother."

Barry continued, "Since the first day here, I have been reading as much as possible in respect to religions, space, time, the universe, and more. Seeing how it takes us back to the beginning, the Old Testament has been the most helpful. The New Testament and Christ's life have proven helpful. As we know, there is plenty of insight into God in both books. Some theology experts believe most, if not the large majority, of the Old Testament was written by Moses. Remember, at the time, as one of Pharaoh's sons, he had the best education available with plenty of time to pen it during their forty years off wandering. A lot like us here, he had personal contact with God. It simply makes sense Moses would be the book's true author up until his death. In the Old Testament, the reader is given at least two stories or incidents where God had taken living breathing human beings into His kingdom for eternity.

"Well, don't you see? We are about to be transported in somewhat the same fashion by God within our tree to another place. This realization does not frighten me one bit, but it does make me think.

"Matt, earlier we discussed free will, near death experiences recounted by the living, our brains, and our souls. Our conversation inflamed the nagging part about all of this within my brain.

"Through science and medicine, we have learned the last part of the human body to die is the brain. So, while every part of our being ceases to exist, our brains are churning. I'd like to know at what capacity. In the interim, where is our soul? Is our soul like a ghost without true form, weight, or substance? Does it rest solely in our brains, or does it move freely within us until the moment all else ceases to exist? After all, everything but brain has died. Is the soul intertwined within the brain and simply composed of tissue, fluids, and energy? So, it would stand to reason the trips have occurred solely within our brains. Is this what God meant through Jesus and the Gospel of Thomas? Literally, is Heaven within us all?

"If so, it would explain the fact God has assured us many times and in many ways he is always with us. Possibly, we are made of God stuff. To me, this would indicate in some small measure, we are God. Within our brains, He and His kingdom are part of us. Maybe, when we are actually dead, God has thrown the switch in our brains to 'replay eternally.' Our last mental experience occurs while in Paradise with our late loved ones? In this plane, time as we know it is suspended. Eternity would have no relative meaning within this context.

"Some have suggested we are all part of the one. There are no new atoms out there. Therefore, are we composed of some of the same atoms shared potentially with Newton, Renoir, Plato, Jesus, or maybe, God Almighty? Is the Creator the original One who has been shared with everyone in creation? Are we of one mind?

"Think about it a second. When each of us entered our Heaven on the initial jump or during any other subsequent trips, how did your loved ones first appear to you — in what form?

"Mine were like moving vapor and without true form. Until they appeared as they had when alive, I could not recognize any of them. But my mind sensed they were. Not one of my relatives who had suffered a long debilitating death appeared to me as they had in their last days. Joining me there, everyone in my family was in all ways absolutely perfect. This is what I saw.

"Can any of you say you saw any of yours in a negative or drastically different way?

"I'll answer this one for you? No. In addition, when we take the jumps or climbs is God bending the space, time, distance, and plane continuums for us? Is he bending the fabric of the universe and beyond for us to travel so quickly, so far, and apparently, so long to find it lasted about a second? Rather, do we actually travel within our brains only the tiniest of distances with time suspended or outright removed from the equation?

"Could all we have experienced, including God and the sum of creation, actually rest on the point of a needle? As you travelled there, didn't you seem small? Maybe, 'there' is the smallest thing in creation rather than the vastness we saw and believed?

"After our work is done, will God decide to allow each of us to ascend while living into Paradise? We've been advised we will perish with Earth.

"These are the things troubling my mind and causing pain in my soul. It is not so much I'm creating confusion as it is I would like to know. Answers are important to me. Yet, since Rod contacted me with this deal of a lifetime, faith has become vitally important to me. So, please forgive me for the rambling and all the questions. It has been great personal therapy to get it all on the table — off of my shoulders."

Jon commented, "Barry, in just a few minutes, you've cleared so many clouds from my mind. They have grown over the last four hundred and fifty years. I have tried to be strong and truck on, as Matt would say. As we face these unknowns together, I'm eternally grateful to have been with you twenty five brothers and sisters. Lucy was right. I had to stay with you, but until this hour, I have not completely been at ease with it. Barry, you have re-moved this doubt from me. I am at peace. Thank you, sir."

Jon continued, "Barry, your words today reminded me of a departed friend, Ernest Holmes. Ernest was an American writer and preacher who died in 1960. We would often discuss many of the same ideas you have given us today. My friend's first book, *Creative Mind*, was published in 1919. Back then, he was instru-mental in forming the *New Thought* movement. He built a church to spread the message.

"In Ernest Holmes book, *Creative Mind,* there is a short pas-sage which seems appropriate for this discussion. It states;

> The way can be shown, but each individual must himself walk the way. We are so bound by suggestion and hypno-tized by false belief, so entangled by the chaotic thinking of the world, thinking which is based upon the principle of a dual mind, that we become confused and are not ourselves. Wake up! Your word is all-powerful, your consciousness is one with Omnipotence. Your thought is infinite. Your des-tiny is eternal and your home is everlasting heaven. Realize the truth – I am living in a perfect universe, it always was perfect and always will be perfect. There never was a mis-take made, and there never will be. I live in the great and eternal universe of perfection from cause to effect, from beginning to end, and "The world's all right, and I know it.
>
> —*The Creative Mind* by Ernest Holmes

"Ernest was a great writer, an excellent teacher, and a powerful preacher. Most of all, he was a great friend. I look forward to our next discussion."

"Jon, I told you Barry and Matt were brilliant, and they would prove to be true disciples," I added.

We all laughed, not a nervous laugh or an uncertain laugh, but for the first time in this experience, we shared a laugh — no adverb or adjective needed.

Before we started the departures, I had one last message... a ray of hope for all, coming to me the previous evening while Jon and I talked with God.

I shared, "As long as there is life, there will be hope. Keep your faith in the One above. We may yet be saved."

Then, one by one they climbed the tree.

The three team leaders went first followed by their seven subordinates.

Within seconds, Jon and I were alone, staring at our garden bench.

We embraced and made a promise to soon meet at his place with Lucy, Patrick, Rose, Faye, and our son. I'll bring Percy and he will have Ricky and Tiny, playing on their farm's rock lawn.

I shook Jon's hand, giving him a firm hug. We said, "I love you," and climbing the tree, he was gone.

I sat on our bench, crying like an old baby, waiting on a miracle.

Streaming Dreams...
Revelations

T he tears trickled to a stop. Slowly at first, I started to nod off. These days, it was nothing new for me. So, I stretched out on the bench with a good rest as my goal. Apparently, R.E.M. sleep had just kicked in, and the dreams were flowing. Ultimately, multiple dreams were presented to me.

First, I dreamed I was awake and staring down at my body. It was as if my inner self, spirit, or possibly, my soul hovered there just above the park bench and my sleeping form. I could see my closed eyes moving quickly back and forth — side to side, watching myself as my body's mind was dreaming something which neither could see. "Bring it into focus," my hovering mind thought. In the muddied dream, I could sense and see my presence on the bench. Apparently, my body was getting frustrated at my lack of attention to these dream events. My hands twitched.

At this juncture, in my voice, I heard, "There will be important dreams to follow — focus and remember." This was a first. I was scolding myself in my dream.

Like one's vision after the removal of two cataracts, my vaporous floating form shot back into my sleeping body. The cloudy veil lifted from my eyes.

The second dream appeared. On our apartment couch, I woke with Randy standing in front of me. Randy was staring at me as he was inclined to do back in the early 1960s. I was a young boy again, and living in the Capitol Homes with my mother, brothers, and sister. Randy was a darling little boy who lived a few apartments away. He spoke every word with a slur, and he was as thin as a soda cracker. He wore his pants and shorts pulled up high on his pale boney hips.

In midsummer in Atlanta, those in poverty knew only one kind of air conditioning, and it was making sure windows and doors remained wide open at all times.

Randy would enter our rear door, allowing the screen door to slam shut every time. Next, you could hear his tiny footsteps in slow shuffle mode, walking to the fridge and opening it. He would retrieve a serving spoon from the kitchen drawer and help himself to heaping spoons of sticky sweet peanut butter, dripping with oil.

USDA government peanut butter came in a non-descript bare metal can with sparse print lettering. Anyone who saw it knew you were poor and on the government dole. A welfare mentality naturally blooms from the years of having to survive on it. Over time, it can become innate. The allure of welfare is almost as strong and natural as the yearly procreation migration events of the penguins, salmon, whales, and other wildlife. We in the condition commonly referred to it as "guv'ment food." My family absolutely loved the guv'ment cheese, peanut butter, and whole cooked chicken with white rice in a can. Without argument, the worst items were the powdered milk and powdered eggs.

I remembered once a month traveling with my mom to a warehouse in southwest Atlanta near Pilgreen's steak restaurant. At the warehouse, the food was dispensed by conveyor line. Once a month each adult received their monthly allotment of food based on the number in their family. We needed two small boxes for five. We were directed, "Grab two boxes and roll along... move on lady, move on." To this day, those uncaring words spoken harshly infect my brain.

In this dream, Randy stood there, licking his heaping helping of peanut butter glued to the serving spoon.

Randy inquired, "Why you ashreep, Rod? Wake up. Rod's ashreep. Lynn's ashreep. Momma's ahsreep, Tim, and David's ashreep. Why's everybody ashreep?"

In a snore, I was dressed and ready to walk to Ed S. Cook Elementary — a long block or two away. As I exited our apartment, I'd always kiss my mom on her left cheek. The kiss would bring red splotches of embarrassment to her face. In deep frog's voice, she'd say, "Get on to school, Rodney." She alone called Rodney. I missed my mom and our six years of almost stable life in the Capitol Homes. The complex was the "hood" of our time.

Next, it was early afternoon. I sat nervously at our rickety kitchen table, waiting for my grandparents, Papa and Nanny, to visit. As always, they came in the nick of time with some much needed groceries and a little cash in hand for mom and us.

The end of each month was the worst for us. Our government dole check came on the first of the month, and the little amount of money lasted about a week.

My Papa and I loved sports. While a young boy, he used to bring me to Crackers baseball games, and prize fights at Ponce de Leon Park. On Friday nights, we used to attend live wrestling at the City of Atlanta Auditorium. If he could not take me, he would make sure to visit us on Friday afternoon, and at the last minute, he'd give me two or three dollars to make the matches. He had a huge heart and a wry sense of humor.

As the rats waddled, the City Auditorium was only about ten blocks away from our apartment. As a seasoned city dweller, you knew how to navigate downtown like the rats. Papa was like a rock... solid as Stone Mountain. Papa was Nanny's everything, and he spoiled her like a child. She wanted for nothing while he was alive.

He was my only adult male role model way back when. I love him dearly. I adore him like a father. He was a kind, generous, caring man, but he did have his limits. He was a man's man in the best possible definition of one. If something was rotten or someone wasn't right in their word or actions as a human being, he could not remain silent. In this respect, Papa reminded me of one person with his character of a movie character in *Gone with the Wind*. If it wasn't fitting, Papa would let you know eye to eye. In all other respects, he was like Spencer Tracy, Humphrey Bogart, and George Bailey rolled into one man. Nanny and Papa were the best.

Then, I saw all the good lifelong friends I had made in those six years of living in the Capitol Homes. Like my initial trip to Paradise, none of the negatives were presented. There was enough of those in reality.

It was a wonderful life.

While within the same dream, I sneezed myself into Heaven. It was like I had been shown. There was a celebration of souls in progress. My loved ones, currently living and deceased, were there. Celestial jubilation covered the entirety of the place.

Its striking similarity to our picnic just the day before did not escape me. Our souls felt like one, but there was knowledge of our bodies. We were perfect and one with God. There was no spinal disease for Faye, no asthma, no severe allergy problems for Rose, and no hideous cancer for mom or Papa. There was no pain, worry, anger, and no envy. He made it known to every soul he was always with us. This was where I longed to be.

The next dream began as quickly as the previous one vanished. Sadness filled me.

This one was different and somewhat of a replay of what we had been shown several times. I was sent back to the previous departure, minutes ago. As the others zipped up into the tree and away, I was shown several endings.

The first was as portrayed earlier the previous evening. Things went as directed by the voice.

The next portrayal differed substantially. The portals were shown in full operation all over the globe. The masses came witnessing for a brief second before departing the area. A massive calendar was shown. The next eight months passed one by one, flipping through calendar. Towards the seventh month, I detected an anomaly. Many across the world were not returning from their climbs. From city to city, hundreds gathered under the trees, and bolts of light could be seen shooting up into the tree and many were gone — not to return.

As I watched my own portal's activities and those of the other twenty five, the phenomenon grew more and more apparent with more souls, making the journey up with their bodies. The sickly, lame, affirmed, elderly, and possible, terminally ill appeared to be those going body and soul in the greatest numbers.

I recalled the earlier conversation by the campfire and what we were told about staying if we desired. In the dream, obviously, this is what was happening.

Next, I witnessed the day of the worldwide warning of our impending destruction disseminated by Jon and me. As directed, we would present the message and the reenactment. Jon began to initiate the message, and as I queued the video, the voice interceded, taking complete control of the audio and video. As he began to address the world, the scene slowly started to fade away... out of focus. The picture I saw became like white noise with static.

This seemed to last only a few seconds when another scene, silent now, started to come into focus as slowly as the last had dissipated. As the scene became clearer, I could see Jon, myself, and the rest of our team seated around my tree on the grass. Again, it was as if I were in two places at once, sitting beside Jon and floating above the group. Within the dream, I was aware I I was dreaming at this point, but the realness of it all was astonishing. I was frozen in its grasp.

193

We were watching the tree while a silent video in washed-out color began to play. A portion of the foliage of the tree became a large white screen. The style of the video was like an old 8 mm family film where the color has faded and any audio has ceased to play. We were shown throngs of New Yorkers while they celebrated the arrival of the New Year at Time Square. The countdown had started. The crystal ball began to move. Midnight and zero were reached. The ball was at rest, and "Happy New Year 2014" flashed across the screen.

Instantly, we were shown a new 2014 calendar. The months began to fly by as each one was ripped by an unseen force from the calendar. They would disappear once discarded.

October 2014 was soon upon us. We were shown scenes of children in Halloween costume, going door to door for their sweet treats. October was ripped and discarded.

We saw November with Thanksgiving Day circled on the paper, and a family was seated at their holiday table in prayer — prior to the ceremonial carving of the golden turkey.

November went and December became the final month, remaining on the calendar. Initially, there was no date beyond the 21st on December's page. As we watched in quietness, the rest of the December days appeared. Both December the 22nd and 25th were circled in red. I smiled. My birthday had been circled, and Christmas was also an expectation.

It was at this moment within the dream, I almost knew, or at minimum hoped, I was correct. Mankind would be given a stay of extinction or a temporary one for the near future.

The screen went white.

A large hand appeared. Three of its fingers and thumb were clasped in a fist, and its index finger was pointing directly to our right. As our attention was directed to the open parcel of the tract to our right, scenes began to appear in spots all across this area of the field. In silence, there were activities representing most of the months of the year. 2015 was shown in a banner hanging above and to the front of the activities.

One family was having their traditional January 1st meal of black-eyed peas, mac-n-cheese, collard greens, baked ham, corn-bread, and iced tea.

Children could be seen delivering Valentine's cards to their classmates in their school.

March Madness was happening, the Collegiate Basketball Championship game was in full motion.

April showers were soon followed by May flowers.

June came around as my family celebrated Rose's birthday.

July 4th was shown. Fireworks lit the sky in its area. Young-sters seated below the explosions quickly concluded a lengthy watermelon eating contest.

August was represented, showing Jon as a young boy, fish-ing from the banks of the Hudson River.

September was filled with football players streaking up and down the gridiron.

October could be seen at the far end of the field with a pump-kin patch filled with customers, thumping melons.

November was the faintest and farthest scene. We could barely see a pilgrim father and son, hunting in deep snow for wild game.

At this point, Thomas shouted, "Where's December? Anybody see December?"

Barry replied, "I think so. Look just to the right of the farthest scene, closer towards the woods. I can see shadows but noth-ing more."

Jim added, "Yes, I see it, too."

When Jim had said the last word, it was over. The field was clear. The screen was gone. The tree was back to normal. We sat there, sharing the same feeling — uncertainty.

In a flash, Jon and I were sitting on our bench, staring at the tree as when we first met some sixteen or seventeen days earlier. It seemed like two lifetime's ago. The twenty four were not present.

Jon said, "There is a message for us." He took a small notepad and pen from his rear pocket, and he started to write. When he was finished, there were five messages provided. By Jon, they were printed as directed. There was one message on each of five pages.

Jon stated, "Here they are."

Stay Your Posts
Look To The Heavens
All Will Be Revealed
Darkness Comes Soon
The Light Which Follows Consumes All

After I had read the last message, I woke in a startle. I was wide awake.

Once again, "Not fair, not fair" assaulted my being.

I had almost slept through my first arrivals. Once I woke, it only took a few minutes for the first of the masses to arrive. Initially, as in a trance, they came. They were ushered beneath the tree by me and simply told to look up.

The end of the beginning had started, but my mind was conflicted by dreams, cryptic messages, and hope.

We may yet be saved!

Also by Ron Shaw

The Yellow Bus Boys
Transmutation: The Life of a Twisted Cop
Mary's Trunk (Cramped Quarters Series Book 1)
Mary's Journey Begins (Book 2)
Mary's Journey Continues (Book 3)
Paul's Story (Book 4)
RED
Dark Tales
The Dead and the Dying
Around The Campfire: Two Badge-Toters' Tales
The Yellow Bus Boys Go Blue: Canada Bound
J
Short & Fun Stories
Without From Within: Poems by Ron Shaw
Dans l'Abime Interieur
Dans l'Abime Interieur Recueil Deux
Dans l'Abime Interieur Recueils Un & Deux
TraVerses: Poems by Ron Shaw
Photography by J. Robert Sosby
Southern Brewed Poetry
Christmas Past: An Angel's Story
Thanks Giving
The Rebooted
Poetry East To West
Novelettes and Short Stories
Uya: A Beast Like No Other

www.ingramcontent.com/pod-product-compliance
Lightning Source LLC
Chambersburg PA
CBHW050735230626
47052CB00002BA/278